The Bookworm

George Genovese

The Bookworm

& other stories

The Bookworm & other stories
ISBN 978 1 76109 306 7
Copyright © text George Genovese 2022
Cover image: Chris Genovese

First published 2022 by
GINNINDERRA PRESS
PO Box 3461 Port Adelaide 5015
www.ginninderrapress.com.au

Contents

Uncle Dom

My Uncle Dom was the bravest man in Malta even though he wasn't a soldier or pilot. On countless occasions, he lamented over his desperate attempts to join the armed forces and how – to his dismay – he'd been rejected. Pointing to the slight hunch on his back, he would say with a disconsolate grimace and drooping head that, being 'a little too unfit and a little too overweight', he was deemed unsuitable for combat. Then, as he rolled his eyes dramatically and looked me squarely in the face, his voice tremulous with emotion, he'd repeat that if fate hadn't so decreed, he'd be out there with the rest of those 'brave chaps' risking life and limb for his country. When he spoke this way, which was quite often, he shook his head with incredulous vehemence so that his fleshy jowls trembled and the folds beneath his chin quivered energetically from side to side as if to reaffirm his disbelief.

Having said this, it seemed as if a burden had been cast off his shoulders (almost like a condemned man who wakes on the day of his execution to find he's been pardoned) and he'd cock his head as if he'd just heard something startling and, gliding his glinting eyes to me, conclude, 'But at least I tried! That's all anyone can ask of a man, isn't it? It doesn't matter, does it, Pep. Everyone does what he can, isn't that so? You know, they say an army marches on its stomach, so being a cook is just as crucial to the war effort as being a pilot…don't you think?'

I loved him, so I had to agree. His contracted brow would loosen and that enormous 'a little too overweight' face relax into a puffy, smiling cheerfulness.

I was five at the time and shared the household with Dom and his adoptive parents, George and Miriam. Now, when Dom would confide his feelings to me like this, sometimes George might walk into the room with a twisted grin on his lips.

What can I say about George? He had served in the First World War in Salonika. He had even distinguished himself and won a medal. He was capable and inventive at whatever he happened to turn his hand to, but the enduring memory I have of him is of someone who went through life with a peculiar dignity – like Dom, tender and sensitive, but with a comfortable and ironic stance that made him reassuring to be around.

Unlike Dom, he was lean and agile, even for his age, and had all the alertness of a rodent. He could sniff out the possibilities of a situation and make sure he turned it to his advantage. Even so, there was nothing selfish in this uncanny ability of his to see himself through any problem as easily as a ferret works its way through a warren to its ultimate goal; rather, he used his savvy as a means of getting what he wanted, and his generosity ensured that the rest of us enjoyed the spoils along with him. When I look back, I think my admiration of his oily mischievousness only came a narrow second to Dom's endearing diffidence.

Anyway, George would interrupt our conversation. Clutching a glass of home-made wine – he made gorgeous wine out of plums, cherries or whatever else he laid his hands on – he'd tell Dom that his problem wasn't his fitness or weight, but the fact that he'd virtually faint at the very mention of a medical examination.

'Yes,' he teased, 'you can't very well face bullets when you go into a funk at the idea of an injection or stethoscopes now, can you?'

Dom would purse his lips, grow red in the face and bluster indignantly that George was being unfair or, with one hand resting languidly on his projecting belly while the other stroked his chin thoughtfully, would counteract, 'A man doesn't have to carry a gun to make a contribution… I do my bit in the kitchen.'

'Ah,' George would retort playfully, 'if we could only get the English to dump that slop you cook on Germany, I reckon we might win this war.' Then turning to me with a feigned whisper while winking an eye, he might add, 'Dom's cooking could very well turn out to be our secret weapon!'

Dom worked as head chef at Dingli Signals Unit and was proud of it. The unit was situated right on the summit of those rugged cliffs rising a sheer two hundred and fifty-three metres above the sparkling Mediterranean at their highest point. At precisely three thirty each morning, he woke up, bathed with the aid of a small porcelain tub by the bathroom mirror, breakfasted and made his way there to begin the day's cooking punctually at four thirty.

In between bombings, he loved walking in the peace of the still and deserted streets, broken only by his echoing footfalls, occasionally savouring a waft of jasmine in the crisp morning air, as he turned over the day's dishes in his mind. Of course he'd more or less worked out his line of attack (which was his way of saying the day's menu) the night before but now in the early morning tranquillity, when, like his thoughts, the island was fresh and calm and seemed a million miles away from the war, he'd meditate over what last-minute touches he might add to make his dishes just that little bit more appetising. He saw his role as a vocation and relished nothing more than when one of those brave chaps complimented him on a job well done, for it reaffirmed the importance of his contribution to the war effort. Lately, though, to his perturbation, he was finding it increasingly difficult to make the dishes interesting as the stores on the island had rapidly depleted.

This was 1942 and the Germans had stepped up their air raids, aiming to force the intractable island into submission. With monotonous regularity, the Luftwaffe ruthlessly pounded that stubborn rock and though morale hadn't yet cracked, an ominous foreboding had quietly insinuated itself into the mood of the Maltese. There was no denying it – the insistence of the raids was taking its toll. The Germans and their Italian allies had effectively blockaded the island and out of the last four convoys from England only a trickle of the supplies needed to maintain its dogged resistance had managed to get through. We were on the point of starvation and with virtually no ammunition to defend ourselves against the supremacy of the Luftwaffe. If a convoy didn't get through soon, we would have to face the unthinkable and surrender.

Dom was by nature an artist who had perfection as his goal. When he wasn't bringing his fussiness to bear on his cooking, it was directed to his other great loves – music and theatre. He could play a wonderful saxophone, which he'd taught himself and for which reason George playfully called him Maestro, but even more impressive than that was his acting ability. He was, in essence, a superb actor. Apart from the rare film at the cinema, which we all loved, the plays put on by the Catholic Action Social Club were the only form of entertainment we had to divert us from the terrors of an oppressive war that no one wanted and everyone desperately longed to forget.

In preparation for these events, Dom often directed, acted, painted backdrops, made props or did all four and much more at once. He threw himself into his work with the enthusiasm of an overgrown child and you could rely on him, whatever the hitches or deprivations, to make sure another successful performance eventuated.

On stage, his hunchbacked figure made a magnificent Iago and it was hard to reconcile Shakespeare's exemplification of human resentment and malice with the pregnant ball of harmless humanity that we all knew Dom to be. And yet such was his acting ability that one cast aside all personal prejudice that might interfere with the drama of the moment and only saw the undiluted malevolence of that character. He was chilling and broke your heart as he wove his cruel web of deceit around the ingenuous Othello.

Everyone sat spellbound during his performances and even I, who had no way of appreciating the complexities of Shakespeare, felt I got the gist of the play as that remarkable aptitude of his spoke to you in a language more potent than mere words. A simple flourish of the hand, a stealthy motion of his ponderous head, and we all thrilled and sighed with wonder as we momentarily lost ourselves in the portrayal of a villain more real to us than even Hitler or Goering. And then, which was the magic of the whole thing, we all walked away from that theatre unharmed and intact, and, more importantly, free to ruminate over the depths of human depravity while knowing we imaginatively stood beyond it. In short, we left the hush of that final heartbreaking scene feeling exulted!

Because these productions of Dom's came out of his true nature and not some unreal expectation of himself – like his fantasy of his being a soldier – he took for granted just how essential they were for our morale. He didn't see that in making a space for our imaginative liberation in the face of overwhelming darkness, he allowed us the luxury of hope at a time when that was needed more than anything. Despite the enemy's attempts to make our fates seem absolutely determined for the worst unless we capitulated, we could walk out from those performances and go home clinging to a belief in our battered independence because, unlike the incensed Othello, so apt a personification of the universal insanity around us, we still possessed the ability to retain some shred of incorruptible humanity. He didn't know it but to me Dom was the best kind of hero – not the kind who sets out to perform laudable deeds, but one who does so oblivious of his generosity.

Even so, his ability as an actor could be unpleasantly overpowering as much as inspiring and he often frightened me as I sat on his knee. He would tell me stories about the viciousness of the Germans. Losing himself in his storytelling, he would give vivid accounts of the enemy's cunning and cruelty so that I grew pale and began trembling. Then (almost ashamed of himself) he'd suddenly notice me on the verge of tears, and, coming back to himself, reassure me that things were not as bad as he had said. He'd stroke my arms and console me that there was no need to worry because he and Uncle George would protect me whatever happened. Still, these stories cut me to the quick because there was one form of entertainment that I relished even more than the theatre and this involved first-hand terror of the Germans.

Often, the air raids happened at night and when they did Aunt Miriam dragged me out of bed, hastily wrapped me in what was to hand and prepared me for the shelter. I hated that, especially when she draped her large black mantle over me, as if it were some kind of protective shield, and guided me blindly through the darkened streets. Now it was pleasantly warm under that mantle and I found the smell her of her body reassuring amid the noise and hysteria, but I couldn't see where I was going and so, apart from being intolerably sleepy, I often found myself stumbling in potholes and puddles down the road. By the time we reached the shelter, I was freezing and soaked all over with muddy water.

Uncle George always stayed in bed, inducing me to protest that I wanted to remain with him. Aunt Miriam would thump him while screaming that there was a raid on. He ignored her and the blaring sirens. Then when she'd cry that one day a bomb was going to fall right on top of him and good riddance, he'd draw the blanket up over his head and mutter that if he were going to die he'd much prefer to do so comfortably in bed than on his way to the shelter. I agreed and envied him for his comfort.

Meanwhile, Uncle Dom scurried around exhorting us to hurry for dear life's sake. In a panic, he'd storm out of the house and, realising he was alone, rush back to collect us. 'C'mon, let's go!' he'd cry.

'I'm not ready!' Aunt Miriam snapped back. 'If you want to go, just go!'

His body would instinctively lurch forward to go. Then, turning his head towards Aunt Miriam and me and shuffling nervously on the one spot like a man standing on hot coals, he'd wipe his sweaty brow with a handkerchief and reply, 'I can't let you go unprotected now, can I?' Finally, shivering all over, he'd lose control of himself and force us both out of the door with my aunt arguing and cursing all the way to the shelter.

The night would pass there to the restless screams of hungry babies and the gloomy murmur of voices as people said their rosaries.

But sometimes, when no one else was around to stop me, I went with Uncle George onto the roof to watch the dogfights. Much as I loved the theatre, that was much more exciting! Most of the aircraft we had to defend us were no match for the Messerschmidts. We did have, however, a handful of Spitfires and it was a different story when it came to those magnificent machines. Somehow, and to this day I still can't comprehend it, they managed to hold their own against the overwhelming might of the Luftwaffe.

We would watch the faster Messerschmidts approaching in packs and then, splaying apart, go screaming in for the kill as they ruthlessly dogged the defenders. Then in a moment of sheer grace, the streamlined silhouettes of the more manoeuvrable Spitfires rose in tight, steep arcs over the preying enemy, sometimes pirouetting like ballerinas and, approaching from his blind spot, swooped in from behind him to his complete surprise. The Germans were determined fighters and had the advantage of numbers so the outcome was by no means a foregone conclusion. But, once the Spitfire had doubled back onto his tail, the German pilot who'd been outmanoeuvred in this way had to be really good not to get strafed out of the sky.

Meanwhile, we saw and heard the howling Stukas, more or less unchallenged, diving headlong with that ominous whine of theirs as they homed in on their targets. It was the memory of that dreadful sound and the daring of those pilots as they swept down like birds of prey out of the sky that piqued my terror when Uncle Dom told me stories about the vicious Germans. You see, unlike the Germans, the Italians, whom Uncle Dom never talked about, remained very high in the sky. Their planes would appear as tiny, silent silver crosses during the day or in the glare of the searchlights at night. While they could be deadly accurate, they just didn't inspire the menacing fury of the Stukas. Where opportunity allowed, the Stukas or Messerschmidts swooped in just above the house tops and strafed anything that moved – man, beast or fowl. I'd even heard of the daredevil antics of some German pilots landing in our very own airfields getting out of their planes and machine-gunning anything in their immediate vicinity before reboarding and taking off again with absolute impunity. If such feats didn't exactly mean we'd been conquered yet, they certainly seemed to imply that day was not far off.

This was all material that filled my active imagination with horror as I listened to Dom's stories, but while I was there actually seeing it with Uncle George, I didn't fear a thing. I sat against his body, feeling its warmth, and enjoyed the spectacle as he vigorously puffed on his pipe or swigged a flagon of wine, occasionally raising his fist in triumph when a defender downed the enemy.

Inevitably, my protective aunt would notice my absence and come to spoil the fun. Her stocky form stormed onto the roof like a black whirlwind (she always wore black) and whining like a Stuka set upon Uncle George. 'Are you mad? You might want to die but don't involve him in your stupidity,' she'd blare as she seized me by the arm. Her big leather handbag would come down in a hail of blows on poor George's head while she continued, 'Fool, mad fool! Why I ever married a man like you is beyond me!'

Uncle George remained unmoved, indifferently fending off her blows while craning his head so as not to miss a moment's action in the skies.

I'd break free and spreading out my arms protectively between her and George whimper, 'Don't hurt him, Aunt, please don't hurt him!'

'Don't hurt him!' she'd scream, as she wrestled me back into her control. 'I'll kill him! Fool, mad fool!'

With that twisted grin of his, George would turn to me and say, 'It's all right, Pep. Now you be a good boy and run along with your aunt.'

In this moment of distraction, she might finally get through his defences and bring down a really good clout on his crown so that George would slump forward and shake his head, momentarily dazed.

Feeling satisfied with this direct hit, she'd drag me away as she glared at him and repeated, 'Fool! Mad, stupid fool!'

All the while, Dom's head poked gingerly around the entrance to the roof while he frantically entreated, 'Are you coming? Quick, it sounds as if they're getting closer. Miriam, Pep, are you coming?'

Not long before the raids finally ebbed into memory, both Dom and George, on the very same morning, had an encounter with the Germans that they often talked about long after the war. George was a stevedore and it so happened that as he was unloading one of the few supply ships that had got through one morning on the dock at the farthest point towards Marsa, it received a direct hit from a Stuka while he was still on board.

When George had collected himself after the initial blast, all he could see was a thick column of smoke and flames rising starkly against the early morning sky. He tried to get to the gangway on the port side but soon found himself driven back by a furious wall of fire consuming the dock. With burning eyes and gasping for the acrid smoke, he stumbled over to starboard with the aim of diving into the bay. When, towards the stern, he finally found a clear vantage point from which he could gauge his chances, he was horrified to see that the harbour was a seething black and hissing ring of fire.

Just then, he heard the desperate screams of his fellow stevedores over the roar of the inferno and, as his eyes adjusted to the lurid glow of the coalescent sea, clearly glimpsed them hopelessly heaving and bobbing in the oily swells amid the shattered and burning flotsam. A tremendous explosion from the direction of the bow shook the whole vessel and showered clanking shrapnel all around him. There was no time to lose. He said a smart prayer, did the sign of the cross and, with his hands sizzling as he clasped the red-hot gunwale of the ship, hopped up on top of it and dived into the churning water.

When George turned up at home that morning, smeared with soot and oil and looking like a bedraggled waterfowl, he seemed unusually pale and gaunt. After my aunt asked him why he was early, his glazed eyes looked at some inscrutable point and he vacantly mumbled that he was damned lucky he hadn't turned up late. We both stood baffled by his uncharacteristic seriousness.

'What's up?' interrogated my aunt harshly.

'I've just seen the gates of hell but the hand of God delivered me,' he said, before absently stroking my head and – astonishingly – tenderly kissing Miriam on the lips. 'I'll explain later,' he concluded as he shuffled to the couch, where he collapsed, exhausted.

Later, we learnt what had happened. As far as George was concerned, his escape had been a miracle. There was no way that he could have swum beyond the reach of that raging slick without divine intervention. It was, he believed, the prayer he had said and the vow he made before he jumped ship by which he'd been delivered or, more precisely, God's trust in his sincerity at that moment.

As it was a Wednesday on which he had come face to face with death, he vowed to God on that sinking ship that every Wednesday for the rest of his life, should he live, he would say the rosary and eat nothing but fish. And for all his irony, for all his stupendous slipperiness, he kept true to that vow till the day he died. Yet, while this fulfilment of his promise always affirmed the true mettle of the man to me, I've often wondered how he would have fared if he'd vowed to give up drinking.

That morning, Dom was cooking in his kitchen as usual. Quite unexpectedly a dishevelled stranger dressed in khakis interrupted him. He looked at the fair, blue-eyed stranger and assumed he was an English soldier or pilot.

'My, my, you're early this morning,' said Uncle Dom, a little startled. 'Just get yourself a chair and I'll bring you some breakfast in a moment.'

The stranger nodded and went into the adjoining room, where he sat amid the echoes of the empty dining hall. Dom came out with sizzling bully beef and military-issue dry biscuits which he'd soaked and mashed with tinned pilchards on a pan, and emptied them onto the plate before the stranger. Because of the stranger's appearance, which looked somewhat haunted and in need of consideration, he even added a fried egg that had been given to him as a gesture of thanks for a favour he had done someone. Eggs were worth their weight in gold, as virtually all of the chickens on the island had been consumed by the starving Maltese, as had the sheep and goats and even horses.

'Oh yes,' he said, raising a reflective finger before storming out and returning with some freshly baked bread.

The stranger gave him an appreciative grin that Dom couldn't fail to notice and wolfed into his breakfast.

Dom returned to the kitchen and pulled out a cigarette from his jacket. He entered the dining hall and sat at the opposite end of the table, where he smoked as the stranger scoffed his meal like a man who'd never eaten. 'Is it good?' he asked.

'Oh yes, splendid…splendid!' replied the stranger as he gulped it down.

The stranger's accent was somewhat unfamiliar but as so many foreign allied troops passed through Malta he didn't give it a second thought.

'It was a horrible raid last night,' said Dom.

'Yes, I know…very scary. I prayed to God to deliver me.'

Dom looked at him inquisitively.

'I am a pilot. I got hit and crashed into the sea.'

Dom's ears pricked up. 'A pilot…crashed into the sea? Well, how did you get up here then, my friend?'

'I climbed up the cliffs,' replied the stranger, scooping up the last of the egg yolk with his bread.

'You climbed up Dingli cliffs – in the dark?' Dom asked incredulously. 'Why, that's unbelievable… No, that's heroic! I don't know of anyone who's done that during the day, let alone at night! You're a hero, sir, that's what you are!'

'No, I am no hero, it was God's doing. I felt like giving up many times but something just would not let me stop and I was scared all the way but, praise God, He saved me. And I must say, now I have met you, I am not so scared any more.'

Dom slapped his brow in disbelief. 'You climbed up Dingli cliffs! Wait on a moment,' he said stretching out his arm. He scurried back with a steaming pot of tea, which he ceremoniously poured into the stranger's cup. 'Have that, it'll do you good.'

The pilot nodded with a smile. He pulled out a soggy packet of cigarettes and said, 'I would like to offer you one for your kindness but…'

'Don't you worry about that. Here, have one of these,' Dom interjected.

As the pilot leaned forward to take a cigarette, Dom noticed something unusual about his hands.

'What's going on there?' he asked, tapping the pilot's hand.

The pilot turned up his palms and Dom was shocked to see that
they were badly gashed and raw with abrasions. Though scabs had
started to seal the wounds, they were still bleeding in places.

'The climb up,' the pilot explained.

'Well, we can't have that!' said Dom. 'Just wait a bit.' He went out
and eventually returned with a basin of steaming water and some cotton
wool and bandages. 'This'll fix you up!' he grinned, squirting some io-
dine into the basin with an eye-dropper.

The pilot studied Dom's furrowed brow and the tip of his tongue
held between his teeth, taut with concentration, as he cleaned his
wounds with all the care and fastidiousness with which he characteris-
tically tackled anything.

'This war,' Dom muttered half to himself. 'So much needless suffering, I'll be glad when it's all over.'

'Me too,' agreed the pilot, 'I just want to go home, be with my wife
and son and work at my trade in peace.'

'Ah, you're a tradesman, are you? What do you do?'

'I am a cabinet maker.'

'I could use a man who's handy with a hammer. I put on plays, you
know, Shakespeare and so forth, for the Catholic Action Social Club
and I'm not bad with a hammer myself, but I can't do everything. It'd
be wonderful to have a skilled tradesman for set design. If you're ever
free, you'd be more than welcome to take part. We don't make any
money but I'd give you a little something for your troubles myself if
that would help.'

The pilot looked at Dom with some perplexity and said, 'No, I
would love to, if I could – you see, I love the theatre, especially Shakespeare – but I do not think they will allow me to do that, will they?'

'Well, I don't know, I suppose you've got more important things to do, but if you have any free time I don't see why it should be a problem.'

'Do you know of Goethe?' asked the pilot.

'Why, of course!' Dom said excitedly. 'I've staged adaptations of *Faustus* many times. It's pure genius!'

Dom had finished dressing one hand when he continued, 'Anyway, my friend, how long have you been in Malta? I know most of the pilots around here but I can't say I recall seeing you before.'

'Just this morning.' the pilot replied.

'You mean you've just arrived here and they're already sending you up to fight the Germans. That's a bit much, I must say!'

The pilot, flushed with embarrassment, leaned back slightly and after a moment's hesitation said, 'Um, you know, I am a German.'

Dom immediately ceased what he was doing and disbelieving his own ears asked, 'You're a wha– a German?'

'Yes, I was raiding the island this morning when I was hit and fell into the sea.'

Suddenly, Dom's eyes fell on the insignia on the pilot's top shirt pocket. Not having looked attentively before, it had appeared to be the RAF symbol of the English pilots but now, on closer inspection, there it was plain as day, an eagle clutching the dreaded swastika in its talons. Dom felt queasy and a horrible sensation running up his spine and all the way to the back of his ears, which were burning, until he felt like he was going to faint. He tried not to betray his discomfort and hastily finished dressing the second hand. Then he poured another cup of tea for the German and said, 'Oh dear, I've just remembered something I've got to do. You just stay here and I'll be back in a moment.'

He got up and made to go into the kitchen when the German said, 'Halt!'

Dom stopped in his tracks and shuddered to the reverberating command in the empty dining hall. He turned round and faced the German, who was staring at him with his piercing blue eyes. The German's right hand slipped down to his holster, unclipped it, and drew out a pistol. Dom's eyes widened with terror. He felt his dry throat tighten, unable to swallow, and his buckling legs about to collapse.

The German smiled, flicked the Luger adroitly in his bandaged hand so that its handle pointed harmlessly to Dom, put it on the table and slid it over to where Dom was still barely standing.

The sound of the sliding gun sent another of those horrible thrills up his spine. He stood there, frozen, struggling to pick it up but the idea of actually touching the glinting weapon was more than Dom could stomach. He stretched out his arms, as if to suggest, 'Now just sit back and relax,' and with a nervous smile said, 'You wait there! I won't be long…'

Next door, Dom made a frantic call to the adjacent barracks, told them of his predicament and implored them to hurry. When he went back to the dining hall, the German was still calmly seated looking at some photographs. Dom took a deep breath and, trying to be as nonchalant as possible, nearly tripped over a chair as he approached him.

'My wife and son,' said the German, offering the photographs for Dom's inspection.

'Mm, she's very pretty,' said Dom.

The German nodded. 'My son is only six months old and I have never actually held him in my arms. I hope that I will not have to wait too long. Even so, I am glad the war is over for me. I am not really a fighter, you know.'

'Well, I suppose sometimes we all get trapped doing things we don't really –'

Before Dom could finish his sentence, five soldiers burst into the hall brandishing their rifles. The German put up his arms and surrendered. They rushed over to him, searched him and were about to take him away when he requested something. The sergeant nodded and the German went over to Dom. He smiled, extended his arm and thanked Dom for his hospitality. They shook hands and before they led him away Dom ran his hands over his apron inquisitively, located something in the vest beneath it and pulled out a packet of cigarettes. He drew three out and gave them to the German. The German nodded appreciatively.

'Well done, Dom, you've just captured your first German. You might get a medal for this,' said Sergeant Wiggins, a lank Englishman known for his pranks about the unit.

'I suppose I have,' replied Dom, flushed with self-approbation.

'It's a good job he didn't put up a fight, though, 'cause we couldn't 'ave done much about it.'

'What do you mean?' enquired Dom.

'We 'aven't got any ammo, mate. Look, all our rifles are empty, but we looked the part as we burst through the door, I trust.'

'So how are we supposed to fight a war without ammunition?' asked Dom despondently as he slumped into the nearest chair.

'It's all right, Dom, we'll get ammo as soon as they unload what's left of last night's convoy. All I'm sayin' is we didn't 'ave any when it really counted,' replied the sergeant.

Dom relaxed a little.

'Still, I 'ope they don't decide to invade or we're done for,' concluded the sergeant with a wink before patting Dom on the shoulder and departing with a smirk.

This was the story Dom first recounted after his meeting with the German pilot. After some weeks, however, various details in his account altered, often with embellishments which grew more and more inconsistent with the initial version, inciting Uncle George to grimace ironically or make sarcastic asides which amused everyone but Uncle Dom.

He would, for example, mention remonstrating with the German, who was intent on resisting to surrender. There was opposition to this idea by the German, a 'contest of wills', to put it in Dom's colourful way, but eventually Dom's forceful and steely-nerved logic prevailed. Alternatively, Dom immediately suspected the stranger and used his guile to put him at ease. When the opportunity arose, he made a grab at his pistol…there was an ensuing struggle…the pistol fell to the floor…he was nearly done for when the German bowled him over…at the last moment Dom managed to deflect his hand before the German could reach his pistol…after much grappling and groping, he knocked him unconscious and called for help. There were countless other versions that I always found much more entertaining than the original story and to me these variant accounts corresponded more closely to my vision of Dom as a hero.

One day while Dom was retelling his story, he had just finished saying, '…and after this colossal struggle, I –' when there was a knock on the door.

Miriam returned to the living room with an English soldier who asked, 'Are you Dominic Vella?'

'Yes,' replied Uncle Dom with curiosity as he ran his thumbs up and down his suspenders.

'Here, this is for you.'

Dom looked at him quizzically.

'I'm Private Stanford from Luqa prisoner of war camp. One of the prisoners made this for you. He's pestered everyone there for a week now and wouldn't shut up until we promised to deliver it to the cook from Dingli Cliffs.'

Inside the package was a beautifully fashioned cigarette case, engraved with a delicate floral border and a vignette in the middle containing a quote from Shakespeare:

> Yet with my nobler reason 'gainst my fury
> Do I take part. The rarer action is
> In virtue than in vengeance.

'That's wonderful,' said Dom, captivated by the workmanship. 'What's it made of?'

'It's from the perspex of a cockpit, a downed Messerschmidt. The beggar's been workin' on it for weeks. Not a bad job. I wouldn't mind one myself. Anyway, he wished me to thank you for your kindness.'

George guffawed and jeered, 'Colossal struggle! We should ship him off to Germany. Maybe his kindness might get Hitler to forget about the war.' He laughed again slyly and swigged from his flagon of wine.

Dom didn't seem to hear him. He just fondled the cigarette case, admiring the craftsmanship with an entranced smile on his face.

Reversal

Emma noticed with increasing interest that since his retirement three years ago, Shane had discernibly changed for the better. He had become very reflective, even philosophical, and much more considerate towards her. As a senior executive, his job had demanded he often spend extended periods away from home that left him little time for domestic or personal involvement. The responsibilities of his role, its attendant stresses, and the sheer lack of shared time available had gradually insinuated a distance between them. It was not an altogether emotional distance, for they still felt tender towards each other throughout their married life, but one resulting from the impositions of day to day practicality, which in her case necessitated juggling her career with bearing the brunt of bringing up their children.

Retirement had proved good for both of them for now they had nothing but time and they were forced to re-establish connections that had remained dormant for much too long. Now that the children were independent, it was almost like when they first met, living for the day and each other without extraneous interferences. Yet, though they had now settled into their leisurely routine, there was something about Shane's bearing that concerned her. At times, he seemed restless, troubled, or even haunted by something she could only indefinitely surmise.

In between helping with the daily chores, Shane was able to indulge a new-found passion for gardening. He'd wake early and spend much of his day working off his restlessness there. That's where he was at the moment and as it was approaching ten o'clock she thought she'd take him a late breakfast and share it with him on the patio. She called him over and after a few finishing touches to the bed he'd just prepared, he washed his hands under the tap and strolled over.

'Oh, Emma, you didn't have to do that!' He nodded to the breakfast.

'That's why I did it, Shane,' she replied graciously.

'Well, thanks anyway. It's just what I need.'

'The dahlias are looking magnificent, as are the roses. You certainly have a deft hand for someone who never took an interest in gardening until quite recently. Look at the way you've shaped those roses. I only ever succeeded in mutilating them with my pruning attempts.'

'Oh, it's nothing, pure luck…'

'Don't depreciate yourself, Shane. You're always doing that these days. That's not the way you used to be…'

Shane's brow creased furtively and he looked away, seemingly to assess his work while he chewed on some toast, but he did so to avoid having to think about his past. Emma's generous appraisal of his skill, or any compliment, sat uneasily with the memory of the man he'd gladly left behind.

Emma had noticed this type of evasive behaviour of late and expected just this reaction. She remained silent for some moments and then said, 'What's the matter, Shane? Is something troubling you?'

'No, nothing…'

'You know you had another restless night last night. Your dreams seem to be quite distressing to you and you talk in your sleep.'

'Me, talk in my sleep? What do I say?' he asked worriedly.

'Well, nothing that makes any sense, but it's clear you're not having a comfortable time of it.'

'Nothing that makes sense, hey?' he said with relief.

'That's not the point! Somewhere inside you there's something that's trying to make sense and I'm sure you can't be thoroughly unaware of it.'

He averted his eyes from hers.

'I've always been of the opinion that people who talk in their sleep are trying to work something out and looking for a way to state it, either to themselves or someone else.'

'Dreams are meaningless. People make such a big deal about them, as if there's some deep dark truth about ourselves they contain. I'm sure they've nothing to tell us that we don't already know…'

'Isn't that what I just said – that you can't be thoroughly unaware of what's troubling you in your sleep?'

Shane felt annoyed at himself. He had been trying to deflect any interest in the topic under discussion but had, as Emma so logically pointed out, contradicted himself by indicating the opposite of what he'd intended. He brooded silently as he felt Emma's sagacious eyes linger on him.

She felt his discomfort and mercifully drew them away as she superficially commented on how beautiful and fresh the sunny morning was, remaining silent as she left Shane to ruminate without disturbance. She could see she had touched on something at that moment and it looked as though he was struggling to find the words to frame it.

'You're right, I have been feeling uneasy of late but it's nothing… I don't know why but I feel like – now you won't laugh at me, will you?' he procrastinated.

Emma grimaced dismissively as if to indicate that nothing could be more preposterous than her reacting flippantly if what he had to say concerned his welfare, as she suspected it did.

'Okay then, I feel like I'm being dogged by something, like I'm being shadowed and as though some disaster might happen…'

'Well, I suppose we all feel a little like that at times, a little apprehensive about what the future might bring, especially at our age…'

'No, Emma, this is almost palpable, like there's someone right here, right now, nearby, taking stock of everything I do, wanting to discover everything about me and lay it bare in all its clinical ugliness for the world to see. It's like those dreams I'm having. I'm always being followed by a sinister shadow growing in size as it nears me. The more terror I feel, the slower my pace gets until I can't walk at all and freeze, stuck, unable to run away. I try to scream but I can't. But, you see,' he concluded elusively, 'it's as I said, I'm aware of that in my waking life, so the dream tells me nothing at all. It just puts that feeling into images…'

'I wouldn't say nothing at all, Shane. The question is why you're feeling that way and if you can get a sense of that, then maybe your dream might have something important to say. It might even be helpful to you.'

Again, Shane felt that Emma's observations were leading him in a direction he didn't want to go. He had hoped that in mentioning his dream as a concession of something tangible, albeit opaque to her curiosity, she might falter against its impenetrability, forcing her to desist, or perhaps agree that what he feared was nothing and he therefore had no reason to be feeling that way.

'So why do you think you feel that way, Shane?' she asked, to his dismay.

'I have no idea…' he answered evasively.

'Don't just dismiss it out of hand, think about it…'

Shane sat in silence for some time as Emma waited patiently, pretending to concern herself with the magazine she had brought out so as not to interfere with what might emerge from his reflections. He looked down at the table sadly and seemed to grow tearful as he tried to speak. Emma felt a sympathetic stab in her heart for him as she cast a sidelong glance but knew this was not the moment to interrupt whatever distress was welling up inside him, much as her protective instinct wished to console him.

'Okay, okay,' he said. 'My worries aren't about the future, not directly anyway, and only insofar as they may affect you, us. What I'm feeling and what I think that dream is referring to is really more about the past. The shadow is my past and, yes, I suppose that may affect our future. I've…er… I've wanted to tell you something for a long time but haven't known how to quite…er…'

She poured him another cup of tea and casually said, 'You've been stuck, dear, unable to find the way to free yourself from your fear, from what you're feeling, by putting it in words, even though you feel it closing in on you in your procrastination, like in your dream.'

He looked up at her with surprised recognition. 'Yes, that's right, exactly right!'

She smiled at him gently and invited him to go on.

'Well, you see, before I retired, my work, the stress, frustration, the whole damn pressure of wanting to succeed and the equally important need to run away from it all, from myself, my responsibilities, and seek relief… When you're so far away from home, so isolated, and everything else is swallowed up by this consuming ambition to come out on top, to avoid failure, you slip up, you falter, and where you succeed in one way you fail in another, though you never see it that way at the time. Well, that…all that… Damn it, Emma! The loneliness got to me…the loneliness…' his voice faltered as he pulled himself back from the brink of breaking down.

Emma reached over and stroked his hand reassuringly. 'It's all right, Shane, go on…'

He groaned, raised his hand to his forehead and sniffling with anguish and shame said, 'I have to say it and it kills me to but… I've been unfaithful to you, Emma, betrayed you…many times…'

Emma extended a plate decorously to him and asked, 'Would you like another piece of toast?'

Shane looked up at her incredulously, automatically took a slice and, at a complete loss to know what to do next, bit into it with utter bewilderment. Amid the ensuing silence, he heard the sound of crunching toast as he chewed on it reverberating in his baffled head. A moment later, he spat it out onto his plate and asked, 'Don't you know what I just said?'

'Yes, darling, I do and I'm grateful to you for telling me.'

Shane rubbed his hand over his blank face looking as if he had just awoken and was trying to make sense of a world still blurry in his grogginess. He was about to speak when he scratched the top of his head distractedly, uncertain how to proceed. With renewed determination, he raised his index finger as if to emphasise an important point he was about to make and then withdrew it, falling into silent perplexity. He looked at Emma as she continued to nibble on her toast and study the magazine at her elbow. 'Grateful!' the word escaped him with disbelieving petulance. 'What the hell does that mean? I tell you I've been unfaithful and you tell me you're grateful!'

'What you feel about your disloyalty is obviously more world shatteringly important to you than it is to me, Shane.' She smiled with unruffled equanimity. 'And you know,' she continued, 'isn't it good you brought up that dream, because everything's exactly like it said, perfectly true.'

'What do you mean?'

'I mean, the more you dreaded getting this off your chest, the bigger the shadow became and the bigger the shadow became, the harder the words you needed to say it – your inability to scream – seemed, but now you've said it there's no shadow between us and I'm glad. You see? You were making something bigger than it really was.'

'Now hang on, Emma, just hang on, this doesn't make sense. I thought you'd break down devastated by my infidelity or even arc up with a perfectly justified murderous rage or something. You're not behaving at all like I expected, not the way any cheated wife should behave. Why, your geniality is perfectly disgraceful! Don't you even feel the slightest resentment at my selfish behaviour, just the tiniest desire for vengeance? For God's sake, please say you do…'

'What good would that do?'

'What good? What about all the guilt and remorse I've put myself through for the hurt you've suffered through my callousness? At least all that suffering, all those secret recriminations against myself would be worth something if you detested me, otherwise I've suffered needlessly and that makes me feel just plain stupid!'

'Well, first, I've suffered no hurt through your actions and you certainly shouldn't feel stupid. As for your guilt, that is a little silly, dear – if you're going to seek comfort or pleasure in anything, whatever it may be, don't explain it away with moral fictions but appreciate it for the good it does you when you most need it.'

'I can't believe you're being so calm about all this. Now don't get me wrong, Emma, I appreciate the generosity you've shown me, truly I do, but I don't care what you say, what I did was wrong and I'm not going to let myself off the hook that easily. As a long as I can, I'll hang on to the remorse that cripples me in the hope that I can come out a better person at the end of it.'

'Shane, you already are a better person, and anyway, I've known of your unfaithfulness for many years now and I'd adjusted to it. So, you see, it didn't cause me the slightest inconvenience.'

'You've known?'

'Yes, you remember Doreen, that muckraking busybody who lived down the road? She'd seen you getting intimate with someone and told me, all out of concern for my welfare, to put it in her weasel words, but really just because she resented seeing anyone happier than her miserable self and, as she was, just champing at the bit for the chance to spoil the prospects of anyone who might be happy. Well, I didn't give her the satisfaction and made a point of folding my arm in yours and smiling deliriously with conjugal bliss whenever she happened to be about. Thank God she's finally dead and buried, the old bag.'

'Ah, I often wondered why you suddenly did that… So you knew, even then.'

'Yes.'

'I'm feeling even more foolish, exposed, now than when I made my admission.'

'Well, don't! Truth is, you did me a favour and I thank you for it.'

'Well, I'm glad I finally 'fessed up, I'm already feeling better about myself but I'd hardly call it a favour.'

'No, I don't mean your owning up, appreciative though I am for it. I mean your unfaithfulness did me a favour.'

'Hey, come again?'

'You know, Shane, I'm just like you, a creature with passions who feels fear, desire and loneliness.'

'Of course, I know that!'

'You were my anchor, Shane, all I ever knew. How old were we when we married – me nineteen and you all of twenty? How innocent we were. When your career took off and you set off on your personal adventure with all of its errant escapades, I started going a little adrift myself. You have nothing to feel ashamed of, take it from me.' Emma lowered her head thoughtfully and sat with her chin in her hand for some time. She raised it smiling and said, 'Shane, you'll always be my first love, irreplaceable, but the favour you did for me was to free me to find another kind of love.'

'Another kind of love?' he said with trepidation.

'Yes, I had long and torrid affair myself…'

'You, Emma. I can't believe it! No!'

'It's true.'

'It was revenge, wasn't it, for my infidelity? I can understand that and even forgive it.'

'Shane, maybe there was a moment of anger when I found out, maybe there was a fleeting wish of getting even, but no, it wasn't revenge. Some women do that sort of thing for revenge but most of us just want to believe we're still desirable, still adorable enough to be loved. I've never felt the remorse you feel and I can only put it down to the fact that there was genuine love in that relationship and there's nothing shameful in that. You were away so often and I was lonely. I so missed the glow of your loving gaze, Shane… Yes, I knew you were unfaithful at that time but that was not an excuse I used to justify myself. It was just the way things worked out, circumstances. There just happened to be someone who was very caring and as desperate for love as me and…one thing followed another…'

'Well, I'll be…and all this time I've been grilling myself over hot coals for nothing. Why are you smiling like that?'

'Ah sorry, love, not for your pain, believe me. I was just thinking how wonderful love is, the most wonderful thing in the world. There's nothing like that feeling of falling in love, your sensitivity to everything, its freshness, the loved one constantly on your mind and even all those silly love lyrics you hear on the radio perfectly true in every sense…'

'Well, I'm very happy for you and your treasured memories!'

'Come on, Shane, don't be like that. Then again, no, keep that – it's nice to see something of your old irascible self returning.'

Shane relaxed and smiled. 'Yes, it's nice to feel on the front foot again, like I can be outraged at someone else's bad behaviour for a change and free of my remorseful straightjacket, however briefly that may prove.'

As Shane eyed Emma, he wondered at just how little anybody really knows another person. He would never in all his days have suspected her of infidelity. She had always been so modest, naive, in his eyes and even pure to the point of awkwardness in matters of love.

'Emma, you're having me on, aren't you, just getting a little well-deserved payback on me?'

'That's just your masculine vanity wishing that were the case.'

'But to me you've always seemed pristine, innocent…'

'That's a misconception of yours I've always puzzled over and I've come to the conclusion that you and perhaps most men seem to have a double image of a woman in your head you can't reconcile. On the one hand, she has to be the pure nurturer who's there just for you and your nourishment and doesn't have any needs of her own, certainly none so basic as her own desires. On the other, she's the dark seductress of nothing but illicit desire inciting you on to adventures of conquest. Well, you'd already conquered me and, being the driven man you were, it stands to reason you'd set out on other campaigns of conquest. As I said, a woman needs to be loved and that's when the dark seductress comes out in us,' she tittered girlishly, 'and a man needs to be acknowledged as powerful, potent, and that's when the conquering hero comes out in him. They're just two different kinds of power, I suppose.'

'A double image indeed! What are you talking about? You've always been number one to me. All those affairs were just diversions.'

'Well, it wasn't pure diversion for me, though I admit there was a little bit of that,' she said with a mysterious arch of her eyebrow.

Shane didn't know how he should feel at that moment. Should he feel betrayed? Should he be angry? Should he feel duped, self-righteous, sad, confused – well, that he was! – trumped, tricked, foiled, outfoxed or just plain happy that the sole burden of guilt had been lifted from his shoulders?

'So when you say it wasn't pure diversion for you, would it be out of line to ask what was special about that man? I say "that man" because I assume this is all past tense, Emma.'

Emma cast her eyes pensively down and replied with a tinge of disappointment in her voice, 'Yes, past tense…all past. He's dead now…'

'Oh, I'm sorry,' said Shane with the stock response at such news and for which he felt foolish when he considered the circumstances and realised he didn't really feel sorry at all.

'He was, well, how can one even put it into words? He was completely unpretentious and yet a dashing romantic – sensitive, caring and chivalrous. He really knew how to make a woman feel like she was the most beautiful thing in the world and the only thing that existed for him. But apart from that, he was cultured. He opened up another world of art and ideas for me that was new and exciting. Shane, I was virtually wasting away with boredom in the suburbs when I wasn't just plain exhausted from my responsibilities. And before we got together, what did I have to look forward to – endless trivia on TV about home improvement and a deluge of cooking shows clamouring to convince you that if you kept yourself hedonistically glutted with good food and lived in a renovated mausoleum other corpses admired or, better yet, envied you for, you were somehow supposed to be happy. Oh, the banality of it all! I would have gone mad if it weren't for him. But thankfully I was lucky. I made a true friend who was as rare for the substance of his character as for the depth of his love for me.' She paused and after reflecting tenderly on his memory, swung her head sideways, winked and, clicking her cheek, affirmed, 'Yep, what a gem!'

'Charming…'

'You're not too hurt, I hope? If it's any consolation, I've never stopped loving you.'

'Hurt? I don't know exactly, maybe a little jealous, though I've no right to be… Whatever I'm feeling, I'm god almighty surprised, that much I do know… Emma, would you mind, and of course you don't have to, but would you mind, because I'm burning with curiosity, maybe telling me who he was?'

She crooked her elbow on the armrest of her chair and rested her chin in her curled index finger and supporting thumb, remaining in that thoughtful posture for what seemed an interminable span. It appeared as if she was weighing up the consequences of any disclosure that might follow and this sense of weighty deliberation only succeeded in goading his curiosity. Still fixed in that attitude, she said, 'I don't know, Shane, it's a little tricky…'

'Tricky?'

'Sensitive…'

'Sensitive?'

'And delicate…'

'Well, I'm not going to force you but I'd love to…' His voice trailed off diffidently as his body automatically leaned forward in hopeful expectation of any scrap of a disclosure Emma might cast his way.

It looked as if she was about to speak but then her brow creased ever so slightly and her index finger uncurled and crept across her lips. With instinctive sympathy to this gesture of kept counsel, Shane's body leaned back in its chair in flaccid disappointment.

A moment later, her finger descended back under her bottom lip and a look of resolve glinted in her eye. Shane's body leaned forward with taut anticipation. But then again her finger crept over her lips as she pondered and again Shane's body relaxed back into its chair. This mutually unconscious choreography played itself out a number of times but finally her finger came to rest beneath her bottom lip and a look of determined and imminent disclosure lingered in her eyes. Shane's anticipation piqued to fever pitch.

'Okay,' she said. 'It was Bernard…'

'Bernard? Who the hell was Bern–'

'Oh, come now, Shane, how many people named Bernard do you know?' she interjected.

It was almost as if Shane hadn't heard, hadn't wanted to hear, the name at first but now he suddenly registered it and reeled back aghast at the revelation. 'Bernard! My supposed best friend –'

'And colleague,' she added as she nodded slowly, closing her eyes deliberately with the anticipated ramifications of her admission, 'the very same.'

'I can't believe I'm hearing this! Emma, please tell me I'm dreaming.'

'Shane, you're dreaming – if you expect me to lie to you.'

'God! Bernard, you dirty old two-timing son of a bitch!' he said, getting up from the table and pacing backwards and forwards with clinched fists in his pockets.

'Now, Shane, don't talk about the memory of your best friend like that.'

'His memory! I'd like to graffiti it with obscenities! Why, I'd ring the little weasel's neck if he were here right now!'

'And what good would that do?'

'Maybe none at all, but it'd certainly make me feel a whole lot better! Why, the slippery snake, you know he never let on about anything like the double life he was leading, not to anyone. He never talked about sex when I tried to wheedle out what made him tick in that department. He didn't even joke about it when the guys at work got bawdy. He was always just plain, drab, respectable Bernard. Yes, ever dependable, grey, boring and – at last an interesting epithet – supremely conniving Bernard! You know, I used to feel sorry for him, always alone like he was. Well, hasn't he had the last laugh?'

'I'm not surprised he didn't indulge in any of your blokey crudity. He wasn't that way inclined and thoroughly sincere in his feelings. It was love and a spiritual thing between us. And Shane, try and understand, it wasn't as though he didn't suffer for our liaison. It hurt him for your sake, and it's not as if he were laughing behind your back, it's just that it was irresistible, for both of us. He always spoke of you in the highest terms and I would say loved you for a friend as much as you loved him…'

'Well, bully for him…' Shane needed time to process the shock of what he had just heard and became engrossed in his thoughts. Eventually he looked up and asked, 'So when did this all start, Emma?'

'It was around the time you both went for that managerial job which accelerated your career and necessitated all those long trips away from home. In a funny way, getting that job was the catalyst for a situation that worked out very nicely for all of us.'

'How so?'

'Well, Shane, you got the well-paid promotion you so desperately wanted and Bernard got me…'

'Perfect,' he said sardonically. 'And there I was consoling the bastard because he came off second best. Jesus, the grotesque irony of it!'

'Shane, I can honestly say on his behalf that he was sincerely happy for you. He never felt bitter or resentful at your getting what you wanted over him.'

'Well, that all depends on how you define getting what you want now, doesn't it? It seems to me he didn't too badly himself.'

'Don't be bitter towards him. In many ways, Shane, he was like a second father to our children.'

'Oh, so I've been an inadequate father too now, I suppose…'

'No, that's not what I meant. You were busy working for all of us. It's just that, well, a lonely woman with young children appreciates a caring man around for them. He looked out for them, took them out, played with them and loved them like his own and that's something we both should thank him for. They all still think fondly of him to this day.'

Shane stopped dead in his tracks, turned abruptly and sat at the table with an apprehensive look on his face. 'Emma, I want the truth now,' he said with a nervous gulp. 'They are all our children, aren't they?'

'Well, of course they're all our children. How could you even think such a thing?'

'Okay, okay, no need to get riled up. But you can't blame me. Until this morning I couldn't have dreamt you capable of taking another lover.'

'Lovers, dear…'

'Lovers! Oh God, this is too much! Now I know for certain this is no dream – it's a bleedin' nightmare… You mean there were others?'

'Only two…'

'Oh, only…!'

'But they weren't important. You and Bernard remain the only two real loves of my life.'

'Oh, thank you very much, that's really reassuring!'

'When I said before, obliquely, that perhaps there was a little diversion involved in my romantic dalliances –'

'Cute euphemism for adultery,' he interjected.

'Shane, if you don't want to hear this, I'll stop right now.'

'No, no,' he recollected himself. 'I do, Emma. Please go on.'

'Where was I? Oh yes, when I said there was a little diversion in my romantic dall–, infidelity, I was referring to those two others. That's all they were to me, little diversions…'

'So who were they? Anyone I know? No one as insignificant as perhaps a brother of mine or something like that, I hope?'

'No need to be sarcastic, Shane.'

'Sorry…'

'Don't be. Nice to get a taste of your acerbic wit again. I think this conversation is doing you good.'

'Yes, like a dose of castor oil or Epsom salts…'

'They were men I just happened to meet casually. I was lonely and they were cute, nicely built. They took the initiative and I responded. But on my honour, only because both you and Bernard were absent for extended periods, otherwise it wouldn't have happened.'

'It's okay, Emma,' he said, waving his hand, feigning to refuse any suggestion of impropriety in what she was saying. 'I know you've always been a woman of principle. But who were they?'

'One was just a plumber who came to do some work on our – oh really, Shane, do you need a blow by blow description?'

'No, I suppose not.' Shane fell silent and after a moment asked, 'But hey, didn't you ever feel guilty about those two physical and obviously less than spiritual flings, or maybe I should say dalliances, to put it in your charmingly harmless way?'

'No, why should I?'

'I really don't know how a woman's mind works. Didn't you say before that in the case of Bernard it was true love, sincere, and therefore nothing to feel ashamed about?'

'Yes, that's the gist of it.'

'Right, that I can understand! But you've just admitted that those two flings were just that, purely physical, and yet you never felt any remorse for them when your husband was tirelessly slaving away for your and his children's upkeep?'

'Our upkeep wasn't the only thing you were keeping up,' she said wryly.

'Very funny, but let's not stray off the subject. You never felt any remorse for those two flings?'

'Now that you mention it, you know, I don't think I ever did and I admit that is strange. I didn't see the contradiction. Maybe a woman's feelings are just more flexible. But who knows what we secretly suffer at times, especially in our dreams…'

'When I think of the agonies I've subjected myself to, the worry, self-loathing, and you don't bat an eyelid at having a good old romp in the hay with a virtual stranger.'

'I wouldn't put it as luridly as that, dear. It's all a question of circumstances, and we can all be victims of those sometimes. But I'm not making any excuses – I needed to do it for my own sake and sanity. In any case, I never expected or wanted you to feel guilty.'

'Well, Emma, I take my hat off to you. If you're any specimen of womanhood, I'd have to say you've got it all over us, not even feeling the need to indulge the hypocritical luxury of guilt to be able to live with yourself. What a fool I've been.'

He nodded to himself with a kind of resigned self-admission and looked at Emma pensively. She was one of those mature women who still retained much of their former charm and beauty. One just knew by the harmonious splendour of their features that they must have been striking in their heyday and that was how he now remembered her, though he hadn't taken any particular notice in years. Her lily skin was still fine, extraordinary for her age, and her cheeks retained the healthy flush of youth. He looked at her eyes and they still possessed all the clarity and luminosity he remembered, as did her hair, now pure silky white but still as lustrous and full as ever. As his eyes descended on those shapely lips that seemed to wear an irrepressible attitude of subtle and intelligent knowing, he felt drawn to kiss them. It was as if this woman with whom he'd spent most of his life and whose well-preserved features retained their allure had somehow transformed into a mysterious stranger with an exciting secret life he knew nothing about and which held him captive in its fascination. Everything about this enigmatic stranger that inhabited the vaguely familiar body of his wife, from her lovely face to her supple body, exuded an inexplicable radiance he found irresistible.

She looked at him intently as his gaze lingered on her and then he smiled, relaxed. He extended his hand across the table and clasped hers tightly, to which she likewise responded. They sat staring at each other, not needing to speak, much like they had done for countless hours when they first met all those years ago.

'You know, Emma,' he said softly at last, 'I'd quite forgotten just how stunningly beautiful you are.'

'Thank you, Shane, that's very nice of you to say so.'

'And not only that, I never realised just how overpoweringly seductive…'

'Why, Shane, it's even nicer of you to say that! It makes me feel thirty all over again…'

'I'm feeling a little that way myself…'

'You know, Shane, it's getting rather hot out here and I feel like freshening up.'

'Yes, yes that's a good idea, Emma!'

As they got up, Shane added with a tenderness he dissembled as an afterthought, 'Oh, and there's one other thing, I've acquired a new-found respect for Bernard. Whatever else anyone might say about him, he always did have superb taste.'

'I think so,' Emma smiled.

As Shane started to clear the table, Emma turned from the wire screen door and with her back to him cast a glance over her shoulder. Her eyes were like burning glass and glowed with unspoken invitation. 'Leave that for later,' she said as she walked ahead into the house.

Shane dropped what he was doing and followed in a trance, feeling like a nervous youth about to venture into the mysteries of feminine love for the first time. Drawn in her magnetic wake, he caught up to her and placed his hand on her hip, trembling with excitement for the irresistible charms of this woman he felt as if he'd only just met.

Artist

Leonard trembled with excitement every time he thought about his imminent departure. Now that he had got his hard-won placement, he would soon be in Paris studying piano and composition at the École Normale de Musique. He looked about the cluttered room he had grown up in with all its treasured objects, his books, manuscripts and curios collected over twenty-one years, and felt as if they had already started receding into an obscurity that would soon no longer include him. Trying to resist the palpable depletion of his past, he fondled an old seashell he'd collected as a child and thought of taking it with him but then, feeling like he'd somehow outgrown it, as he had the cramped bed he'd slept in all those years, smiled wistfully with a resolve to leave it behind.

He heard the murmur of voices in the adjacent bedroom and tried to be as still and silent as he could amid the memorial ghosts that his room evoked. He lay down on his bed with his head pillowed in his clasped hands and stared into space. A feeling of fear settled in the pit of his stomach as he thought about the challenges ahead for, despite all his brilliance and hard work, he still felt undeserving of the opportunity good fortune had placed in his lap. After all, he was only the product of humble working-class stock, a family that neither understood nor valued the circle of high culture his native ability had thrust him in. Musically speaking, his mother had a lovely voice and loved to sing along with the radio but it was only the disposable popular songs of the day she enjoyed. She was a tender soul, wholly self-sacrificing for her children, who had suffered at the hands of his father and had little joy in her life so that, recalling the brutal humiliations she'd endured, he felt guilty about his secret depreciation of her simple taste and reprimanded himself for his aesthetic elitism. That was always the way with him, torn between an uncompromising devotion to the expression of highest art and a sense of remorse that he was giving himself airs at the expense of the humble people who had nurtured him and made everything worthwhile in his life possible.

His father worked in a canning factory and was affable enough in public but a tyrant at home. He expected everything done for him immediately and had an explosive temper if he didn't get his way. When he was drunk, he could get physically violent, and growing up Leonard was terrified of him, as much for his mother's and brothers' sakes as for his own.

As the voices in the next room sounded softly, he remembered the often disturbing emanations coming from there. As a child, they didn't make much sense but as he got older he understood their meaning and wept helplessly, cursing himself for his cowardly inability to stop them. On such occasions, he could hear his mother say, 'No, I can't.' His father's insistent voice would be heard. 'But no, Harry, no, not now, I've got my...' Then he might hear a slap and the abrupt rustle of linen, as if forcefully thrust aside, followed by the sound of his mother whimpering quietly, suppressing her wish to scream so as not to disturb the household, accompanied to his father's bestial grunting and groaning as he imposed himself on her.

Next morning, his mother crept into the kitchen like a brutalised dog, broken and ready to tremble at the slightest suggestion of its master's hand reaching with displeasure for the nearest stick. Her every inhibited movement seemed almost brittle, as if she might break into pieces if she didn't struggle to keep a dissembled composure. Her eyes were empty, sapped of spirit or any hope of release from her intolerable plight, and betrayed embarrassment for the bruising she tried disguising with make-up. At such times, Leonard would look at his father as he entered the room barking orders with callous self-satisfaction for his breakfast as his mother nervously timed it with his entry and felt a burning rage to avenge her kept only in check by his fear of him.

He lowered his eyes, looked ahead and saw the picture of his cat, Mr Moggins, dead now ten years, wedged between the mirror and its frame. He had loved that cat, as he did all cats, and for Leonard Mr Moggins was one of the rare and beautiful things of absolute joy in what was otherwise a harrowing existence growing up. Popular as he had become with women, for he'd already had affairs with several, and unlikely as he was to settle down with any one of them in the foreseeable future, any relationship with a cat, should he ever get another, would be one of monogamous fidelity and till death do us part, that he knew for certain. He smiled affectionately as he recollected some of Mr Moggins's antics but then winced abruptly and gazed ahead sternly.

His father had made no secret of his antipathy towards Mr Moggins. He would bore everyone with monologues about how useless cats were, how offensive the smell of their urine was by the front door, and a host of other objections that hurt Leonard, the last of which was the inevitable conclusion that as they couldn't afford to keep one anyway something had to be done.

One day, returning from school, Leonard was surprised to see that Mr Moggins wasn't waiting at the front gate to greet him with an expectation of his customary stroke of the cheek as he arched his back with delight and rubbed against his leg. Puzzled by this departure from his routine, he asked for his whereabouts.

'Dead as a doornail by the back fence and good riddance,' his father replied.

'What?' Leonard cried in alarm.

'Yep, I reckon he's eaten somethin' he shouldn't've, the stupid cat,' his father sniggered callously.

'No!' he screamed as he ran to the backyard. There he found Mr Moggins curled with no visible injury but with his eyes fixed in a tortured stare and his mouth agape as though reaching for an agonised caterwaul he couldn't release. Leonard fell to his knees and hugged the stiffening body screaming with grief and heartbreak.

His mother came out and consoled him as he sobbed. Eventually, she said, 'Now, come on, Lenny, let him go and let's bury him.'

He didn't want to let him go, never, but knew his mother was right and immediately relaxed his grip. 'I'll do it, Mum, it's okay, I'll bury him,' he sniffled.

'Good, you do that,' she said, stroking his head tenderly.

As he was digging a hole, his father came out and asked what he was up to.

'I'm burying Mr Moggins.'

'Burying? Ruining my garden for that mangy sack of bones, you mean. What's the good of that? Forget it!' He went to the shed and came back with a hessian sack into which he flung the corpse before depositing it into the bin. 'Now fill that hole up!' he ordered gruffly as he thundered back into the house.

With tears streaming down his face at the thought of poor Mr Moggins's body dumped unceremoniously in a bin, lying there to be thrown away like any piece of rubbish, Leonard felt an unbridled hatred for his father from that day on and wished with all his heart that the hole he'd started digging had been meant for him.

Even now, he could feel a tear running down his cheek as he recalled that torturous event. He never knew for certain if his father hadn't perhaps poisoned Mr Moggins, though he'd often suspected it, but in any case, just the insensitivity he'd displayed towards his feelings and the manner of Mr Moggins's disposal were sufficient to stir up the same unabated revulsion of him as he lay there thinking on the bed.

He wiped his eye with the back of his hand and then his mind took one of those inexplicable turns and from one of the worst experiences he had endured found himself dwelling on one of the happiest, in fact, not merely happy but blissfully life-changing.

He was in his first grade at secondary school. Arriving early to his first music class, he heard his teacher, Mrs Ellis, playing the first movement of the Moonlight Sonata as he stood there spellbound by the sheer beauty of it. He had never been in the presence of an actual piano before and had certainly never heard one played with such skill. As she sat there in a tweed knee-length skirt and white blouse with a frilly laced neckline, he crept up to his new teacher in awe and sat beside her, avidly absorbing what she was doing on the keyboard as his heart pounded with excitement. Having done so, he was amazed at how something like this piece of music that moved from note to note and chord to chord could evoke such absolute stillness, such dreamlike tranquillity and tenderness eloquent beyond words in its sublimity. He felt the vibrations passing through his shuddering body until he found himself softly weeping with joy for each tender stroke of the keyboard, almost expiring for the unbearable sweetness of it and not wanting it to stop. But not only that, he also saw vivid shapes, colours and patterns of indescribable purpose float before him as the music commanded him to listen, realising then that life was not just about meanness and the endurance of oppression but something inherently beautiful and possessed of dignity if only one had the key to grasp it for what it really was in a way in which this musical piece had revealed to him.

When Mrs Ellis finished, she saw him wiping his eyes shyly with embarrassment and asked, 'Is my playing so bad that it's left you nursing your disappointment?'

He shook his head silently and feeling her eyes on him said, 'I've never heard anything so beautiful…'

She smiled a little flattered and said, 'Well, you certainly have good taste and I'm not bragging about my playing either – the credit is all Beethoven's.'

He had heard that name somewhere, but where before it was something vague and irrelevant, he now knew that it was closer to him than anything he had ever known; he knew too then that whoever Beethoven was, he had been there in that room with them and alive through his music.

After class was finished, he asked Mrs Ellis if he could stay through his lunch hour and practise some piano. She looked over from her desk where she was packing her things and said he could as long as he was respectful of the instrument. He had to make sure he put the cloth back over the keys when he was finished and closed the lid. He nodded. The next moment, he started working out the Moonlight Sonata, somewhat clumsily at first because he had missed the opening bars and his fingers were untrained, but as he persisted, his playing became smoother and more expressive.

Mrs Ellis put her books down and walked over to the piano. She listened to him with interest, occasionally nodding with approval. When he finished, she said delightedly, 'Ah, so you've played a bit of piano before!'

He looked up shyly and responded, 'No, Mrs Ellis…'

'No? Not at all?' she asked with surprise.

He shook his head.

'Then, how could you do what you just did?'

'I watched you,' he replied.

Her eyes widened with a sort of baffled and pleased sense of discovery and she smiled warmly at him. 'Well, my good man, from now on you are going to play it – and regularly!'

He looked up at her appreciatively and returned her smile with an indescribable feeling of happiness.

As he didn't have a piano, Mrs Ellis devoted her lunch hours to his tuition. She was astounded by his rapid development and particularly with his phenomenal memory. After one particular session, she said with a troubled look on her face, 'This is not good enough!' and he, thinking she was referring to his playing, promised that he would work even harder. She looked at him with her large, sensitive eyes and the tension in her face relaxed as she said, 'No, that's not what I meant. It's just that you deserve more time…'

He was puzzled. What more could he do than go home and play all he had learned over in his imagination with the keyboard assimilated in his head? Though he could only hear the notes faintly, he could imaginatively coordinate a visual memory of the keyboard with the distant sound of the notes he heard internally and this he did – constantly.

The next afternoon after school, he realised the meaning of Mrs Ellis's inadvertent utterance which had perhaps escaped her as she considered how best to tackle what bothered her.

She knocked on the door of his parents' house and introduced herself. She only needed to say, 'I need to speak to you about your son,' for there to be an undercurrent of hostility, especially on his father's part, because teachers only ever visited a child's home when there was trouble. 'Your son,' she continued, 'has the makings of a virtuoso pianist and we need to give him special attention…'

They didn't quite know what virtuoso meant but judging by the look on her face as she continued to speak, warmly and enthusiastically, they surmised it probably didn't mean trouble.

When Mrs Ellis looked at his surly father and sensed the uninviting, though tidy, atmosphere of Leonard's environment, she knew she had arrived on the scene in the nick of time. 'With your permission,' she said, 'I would like to take him home with me some nights for piano lessons, and personally bring him back safely when we're done. Your son has incredible talent which shouldn't be squandered.'

When his father realised there was no imminent fight to be had with some uppity woman teacher, he lost interest and waved his hand indifferently, saying, 'Aw, do what the hell you like with him.'

His mother, on the other hand, was concerned. How could she ensure his welfare after hours when she wasn't around?

Mrs Ellis smiled with immediate sympathy and assured her that as a mother herself, she understood her qualms but insisted that her son was special and really needed extra attention to bring out the best he was capable of.

As his mother stood there silently, Leonard begged her to let him go with Mrs Ellis because he knew (especially since he had improved so much under her tuition) that she was his only hope of fulfilling what he now most wanted to achieve in life.

Scrutinising Mrs Ellis carefully, his mother could see she had Leonard's welfare at heart and nodded in assent, proud that such an obviously refined and educated woman like her would take an interest in her son.

Before she left, Mrs Ellis cast a sidelong glance into the smoke-filled lounge room in which his father sat sullenly listening to the horse races on the radio guzzling beer and pressed his mother's hand saying, 'Look, if you ever feel like talking or having a cup of tea, please drop in.'

His mother nodded meekly.

Leonard suddenly grasped the connection between the two memories his mind had flicked between. Though they were opposites in emotional extremity, they both found a release in tears, one in tears of anguish at the death of his beautiful cat and the other tears of joy upon the discovery of music, both being two expressions of the same thing – a beauty so fleeting and intense it was painful.

At Mrs Ellis's house, Leonard felt like he'd walked into a new and mysterious world. It was a sumptuous world full of colourful paintings on the walls and a library of books that stretched across the lounge room wall. There was beautiful antique furniture of rich dark wood, and comfortable lounges of well-worn leather. But most impressively, his heart jumped with joy to see a baby grand in Mrs Ellis's study. Before being invited there, he could not have imagined a place so warm and comfortable, so safe, in which the residents, Mrs Ellis, her husband Chris and their daughter Harriet, could not only follow their intellectual and artistic pursuits free of harassment or disturbance but actually encouraged each other to do so. This felt like a real home to him and he had to get used to the casual friendliness and consideration shown towards him, especially by Chris.

On that first day, before they'd started the lesson, Harriet poked her head into the study and asked if she could say hello to the new pupil. She was a pretty, free-spirited girl Leonard's age with a round doll-like face, big eyes and cherry-red lips. Leonard immediately liked her.

She went up to him and said, 'Mum says you're a gifted artist.'

He was surprised and even embarrassed, because he didn't think of himself that way at all and wasn't quite sure what that exactly meant.

'I'm an artist too,' she said with unpretentious directness as she extended her hand to him. 'Maybe one day we could work together...'

She smiled and exited, upon which he asked Mrs Ellis if her daughter were also a musician.

'No,' said Mrs Ellis, 'her medium is paint and light. A lot of those paintings on the wall are by her.'

Leonard was impressed, because he had liked the ones he'd glimpsed on the way to the study.

'But you know, Lenny, in some ways what she does isn't that different to us because in the end it's all about form, feeling and colour but, most importantly, getting all those things into balance for the effect you want to achieve. Take my husband Chris, for instance. He's a poet and he paints with words by bringing out the music in them.'

He hadn't thought about it that way before – that you could paint with music and yet he distinctly remembered seeing shapes and colours when he'd first heard Mrs Ellis playing the Moonlight Sonata. He realised too when he had learned the name of that piece that the sublime stillness of the first movement was just like an absolutely tranquil body of water over whose surface the moon glanced and flickered, here and there, ever so delicately, perhaps as some solitary figure stood in a wondrous landscape contemplating the splendour before him and overcome with tender suffering and longing amid the fragile hush.

'Now, Lenny, I want you to have a go at this piece…'

'Yes, Mrs Ellis,' he said as he prepared to begin.

'But first there's just one rule you'll have to observe when you're here with me.'

He looked at her.

'Here, we're musicians on equal terms, so just call me Joan. At school it's different, so there we have to pretend to be formal.'

He nodded with a smile to her.

Over time, Leonard felt like another member of the household, free to wander about and look at the paintings or read any of the countless books on the shelves, and in this environment he thrived. His views on things were consulted and accorded equal weight like anyone else's and he was invited to take part in any of the family activities if he desired.

On one occasion, Chris said, 'You know, Harriet, I don't know about you but I need a little inspiration and I want Joan and Leonard to provide it for us. We should pool our resources and have an all-out artistic congress.'

And so Chris orchestrated it so that while Joan and Leonard played a selection of duets, he could sit in a chair and use the music they produced as a prompt for his poetic improvisations while Harriet painted quietly by the window, occasionally glancing studiously at Leonard before returning to her canvas. Leonard easily immersed himself in the congenial atmosphere and felt it was one of the most inspirational days of his life.

At the end of the event, he was surprised when Harriet came up to him with her painting and presented it to him, saying, 'Here, Len, for you, a portrait of a fine artist and gentleman.'

It was an impressionistic picture of him done in one sitting with sure and unerring strokes and signed 'Harriet Ellis 1946'. He had never been so moved and was speechless but eventually found the voice to thank her.

'No need, Len, the pleasure was all mine – you have an interesting face…'

Mrs Ellis had consistently held in check the desire to express her admiration of Leonard's ability because she didn't want to risk his falling into complacency but she had become increasingly aware that his technical mastery had got to the point where it far outstripped her ability to be of any further use to him. She would have to do something soon to ensure his further advancement and this would mean giving up the care of this boy, now sixteen years old, whom she had started to regard like her own child.

She told him one day that he should audition for admittance into the Melbourne Conservatory. He agreed but said that he was expected to get a job soon to pay his way. She nodded deliberately and told him to leave it to her.

Not long after, she visited his home one evening. In her hands, she carried a black forest cake she'd baked covered with brown paper. 'This is for you,' she said to his mother.

She was led into the lounge room, where his father sat brooding over the paper as his mother placed the cake on the table. When it was uncovered, his brothers' eyes lit up with excitement. They had never seen such a delicious-looking object smothered, as it was, in silky cream and sprinkled with flakes of rich, dark chocolate and surmounted with luscious glazed cherries just begging to be eaten. They bustled with excitement as they competed with each other to get the first piece.

'Mr and Mrs Bancroft, I hope I'm not disturbing you but I've come here tonight because of something extremely important. I've done about all I can for Leonard, musically speaking, and he needs to get to the next level. With this in mind, I've brought this…' Here, she rummaged in her handbag and pulled out a folded piece of paper. 'This is an application for a scholarship with the Melbourne Conservatory which I've filled out. As Leonard is still underage, I need one of you to sign it so that, should he get an audition and pass, as I'm sure he will, he has your permission to take up his course of studies.'

Leonard could see that his mother wanted to comply but was too frightened to speak of her own accord.

Mrs Ellis sensed this too, upon which she turned squarely to his father and asked, 'So, Mr Bancroft, will you sign it?'

His father was silent for sometime then scratched his stubbly jaw and drawled, 'I dunno. He's not a kid any more and needs to pay his way if he wants to go on livin' here…'

'But Mr Bancroft, don't you see? This scholarship would pay for his education. You'd lose nothing out of your own pocket –'

'And anyway, I'd continue to do odd jobs like I've always done,' Leonard interjected, avoiding his father's eyes and addressing his mother.

'Besides, there's another thing…' Mrs Ellis said with a sense of gravity she purposely hesitated expanding on. When she felt her silence had sufficiently galvanised interest in what she had to say, she added, 'Leonard can earn money from piano tuition, a lot more money than just doing odd jobs.'

'And how's he going to tutor when he doesn't even have a piano?' his father asked mockingly.

'But he does have a piano, a very good one!' she responded to Leonard's father, who looked back at her in perplexity.

Leonard cocked his head in bewilderment and looked at Mrs Ellis. He had in fact been saving for a piano and was just about in a position to afford a cheap second-hand one but hadn't said anything to anyone.

'He has my piano,' she finally said. 'He can tutor from my place. I've got more students clamouring for lessons than I can handle and I'll pass them on to him,' she exaggerated. 'In fact, the demand is so great it pains me to have to turn away so much good money,' she said with a twinge of shame, aware that her exaggeration was fast becoming a total lie.

'Do you really mean that, Joan?' Leonard asked.

'Of course!'

'You mean there's money to be made from all that nonsense?' his father interrupted.

'A great deal of money, much more than as a shop assistant or factory hand,' said Mrs Ellis.

His father again rubbed his face and became thoughtful. 'Well, okay,' he finally said, 'just leave the paperwork here and I'll look it over tomorrow…'

'No, now please, Mr Bancroft, I need to post it tomorrow…' insisted Mrs Ellis, her unremitting eyes burrowing into his father. 'I believe I've got a pen here somewhere. Ah, here it is!' she exclaimed as she withdrew it from her bag.

She extended the paper and pen to Leonard's father and, as he sat slouched on the sofa, he looked a little intimidated by the lean and proudly erect frame that stood over him unmoved by his procrastination.

'A lot of money in all this music stuff, ya reckon?'

She nodded with indubitable assurance as she made a mental note to make confession of her dishonesty before communion next Sunday.

Leonard and his mother looked at him uneasily wondering how he might react before Mrs Ellis's unflinching resolution but they quietly sighed with relief when he took the paper and signed it with what appeared an inexplicable and disarming feeling of compulsion.

Leonard auditioned and won his scholarship. He had spent the night before his first class at Mrs Ellis's. When it was time to go, he turned sadly to her on the doorstep and hesitated.

'What's the matter, Lenny?' she enquired.

He felt torn between a desire to embark on the next stage of his musical career and a sense of loyalty to her. 'I don't want to leave you, Joan. I want to keep taking lessons from you…'

'That's impossible, Lenny. You're far better than I'll ever be and you know it. Anyway, it's not as if we won't be seeing each other regularly – you'll still be giving lessons from here.'

Before he could stop himself, he flung his arms around her and held her tightly in silence.

Mrs Ellis reciprocated but then clasped his arms and gently drew him back, upon which she gazed tenderly into his face and said, 'Leonard, don't ever forget where you've come from and don't abuse your God-given talent. It's a hard old world at times and sometimes you need to push and shove to get your way but where you can retain your humility. Remember, however good you are, there's always someone better you can learn from.' Then, shaking him gently with encouragement, she said, 'Trust yourself, like I trust you. Go out and take what's rightfully yours! Now you'd best be off.'

He walked away fired with self-confidence and burning with zeal to prove himself. As he got out of the front gate, he turned to where Mrs Ellis stood on the doorstep and in the glow of the front light caught her brushing a tear from her eye before re-entering the house.

Melbourne Conservatory exceeded anything he could have imagined. The depth of musical talent of his peers and instructors was astounding and inspired him to work with unmitigated passion. He blossomed like a pot-bound plant suddenly transplanted into fertile ground in an environment where total devotion to musical excellence came first, except for, of course, the welcome distraction of frolicking with the many beautiful female musicians he encountered.

It was there he met Jerry, a pianist four years his senior of comparable ability. Unlike Leonard, he was tall with a manly build and an impeccably handsome face rounded off with a poet's sensitivity women visibly swooned in the presence of. They immediately struck up a friendship and submitted their compositional attempts to each other's scrutiny. He would often find himself shaking his head with disbelieving admiration at some of Jerry's best work, muttering to himself, 'Amazing, brilliant...'

Alongside mutual respect for each other's artistry, there was a friendly rivalry, like a running joke, spurring each to impress and if possible outdo the other with their creative efforts which proved valuable to them both. There was also a social dimension to their friendship as personally advantageous to Leonard as their creative collaboration. In their free time, they would seek out adventures with women together. Jerry's good looks inevitably attracted their attention but it was impossible for them all to have Jerry. This was beneficial to him because he, no less short of charm and now more certain of himself than ever before, found himself surrounded by countless delectable women all ripe for romance and to whom he courteously extended his willingness to oblige.

That first year at the Conservatory had proved eventful in a number of ways. He won a major statewide competition for piano performance. The winnings not only allowed him to replace the old piano he had by then acquired with a superior one, but also made it possible for him to pass on a considerable sum to his mother for his upkeep, temporarily pacifying his father's annoyance that he'd been duped by Mrs Ellis when the flood of money she'd assured him would follow his son's embarkation on a musical career hadn't been forthcoming. His victory had made him known locally, however, and he started getting offers from regional orchestras for recitals and that did supply him with the much needed funds to help safeguard his beloved Mrs Ellis's honour.

But more importantly for Leonard, that was the year something really momentous happened which changed him forever. On one particular day, he had left the Conservatory early because he was feeling ill. When he got home unexpectedly, he could hear his mother in the kitchen screaming in pain. He bolted there and as he stood in the doorway saw his father pulling her hair and berating her for having accidentally dropped his lunch on the floor. With his mouth to her ear, he hounded her about what a stupid, useless woman she was as she stood there helpless in his grip, her eyes locked in a sidelong look of terror for what might follow next.

Leonard cast his books aside and clasped his father's wrist with what seemed prehensile strength in his fury so that his father's hand automatically released its grip. He thrust it aside and shouted, 'Leave her alone!'

His father, at first taken aback by Leonard's audacity, looked briefly disoriented, but then came back to himself with vengeful rage. He moved towards him and growled, 'Why, you little son of a bitch, you're gonna get a good clip over the ear for –'

Before he could finish his sentence, Leonard landed a punch squarely on his jaw that sent him reeling backwards slamming into the wall, against which he slid to the floor to his rump and where he lay dazed from the impact. The crockery on the shelf above him came crashing down and smashed about him. His mother let out a scream and went to the aid of her husband.

In his rage, he paced towards his father, not knowing himself what he might do next, but his mother, by then crouching beside his father, looked up at him and raised a shielding hand, saying, 'No, Len, don't, please don't.'

His mother's terrified reaction jolted him back to his senses and he stopped, shocked by the awful look he'd provoked on her face. Thrusting his finger at his father as he moaned on the floor, he said, 'If you ever touch her again, I swear I'll kill you!'

He stood over them puzzled and even annoyed at his mother's attempts to help his father. He didn't know why she should bother. Maybe she wanted to defuse a situation in which he, himself, might get hurt or suffer in consequence of what he might have done next. Whatever the reason, he knew she was just being her caring self.

As his father recomposed himself, he waved her aside with his arm and struggled to stand in his grogginess. Once he did, he held his jaw and looked at Leonard with a mixture of anger and caution. They stood there tensely eyeing each other until his father cast his eyes to the floor in defeat and left the room.

From that day on, there was no more physical violence directed at his mother, at least when he was around, and his father kept sullenly to himself. For Leonard, it was as if an intolerable burden that had oppressed him as long as he could remember had been finally thrown off his back.

As he lay on the bed, he felt his hand clenched into a fist at the back of his head and a tension at the base of his spine. He relaxed his back and set it at rest against the bed, opened his hand and readjusted his head on the pillow. It was then he realised he could hear a subdued moaning coming from the next room and tried not to listen.

'Ah, Jerry,' he thought, 'what a strangely attractive creature… maybe even a genius…'

He remembered the first day Jerry came to his place. They'd been ribbing each other about who was the better pianist. As they entered the house, Jerry quipped, 'Nah, there's no doubt about it, Len, you're the best player at the Conservatory, teachers included – after me.'

'Oh yeah,' he retorted playfully, 'Well, we'll see about that!'

They decided on a little friendly competition and sat at the piano in Leonard's room.

'Schubert's Fantasia in F minor,' exclaimed Leonard as he set the score on the piano.

'But hang on, that's a duet for the same keyboard –'

'So?'

'Well, if we both play as impeccably as I'm sure we will, we'll have no way of knowing who's better because we'll just be working in tandem to achieve the same goal, if that makes sense.'

'But we're going to play it with special rules…'

'What rules?' asked Jerry.

'No rules…' Leonard smiled.

Jerry gave him a puzzled sidelong glance. By way of example, Leonard began the piece with a whimsical extemporisation of the opening bars but then stopped and looked at Jerry expectantly.

'Oh, I see,' smiled Jerry as he rolled up his sleeves.

They began the piece with all the seriousness the work demands but introduced improvised phrases at various points, to which the accompanying musician had to respond in as coherent a manner he could while keeping intact the overall fabric of the work. They often found themselves nodding in approval or audibly laughing at each other's outlandish inventiveness. As they progressed, their jousting became more phantasmagoric, one might even say perverse, interspersing burlesque flourishes of dance hall cadences, jazz technique and snippets of popular songs while maintaining the recognisable architecture of the piece before them. At the coda, they resumed performing the work as its composer had intended and concluding it faithfully with the rigour it deserves collapsed into a fit of unrestrained laughter.

'Okay, you win,' said Jerry as he chuckled.

'No, you do.'

'Ah-nah, I know what I'm talking about. You outdid me.'

'Are you implying that, musically speaking, I don't know what I'm talking about? You outdid me!'

'Okay, let's call it a draw,' said Jerry as they shook hands with bonhomie.

'One thing's for sure, Jerry, poor old Schubert certainly lost out…'

At this point, his mother poked her head in the door and was halfway through saying, 'What's the hullabaloo –' when she noticed Jerry seated at the piano by Leonard. 'Oh,' she said as she adjusted her hair with nervous surprise.

'Mum, this is Jerry, Jerry, Mum…'

'Oh, pleased to meet you, Mrs Bancroft,' Jerry said as he got up to

shake her hand. 'I…er…study music with your gifted son over there…'
he said. As he continued to hold her hand, he added, 'We were just
playing a friendly game to see who could best deface Schubert – quite
a feat when all our instincts strive for perfection…speaking of which…
er…I'm very pleased to meet you…'

She smiled as she continued staring at him until, realising she was
doing so, retracted her hand and nodded shyly in acknowledgement of
his compliment. Suddenly, she seemed self-consciously awkward, running her hands nervously down the side of her dress as if to straighten
it or maybe just keep them occupied. 'Sorry to barge in on you like this
but I was just making a cup of tea. Would you like one?'

'Yes, Mum, we'll be out there in a minute…'

As she closed the door behind her, Jerry stole a look at her and met
her furtive glance cast back at him, upon which she lowered her eyes
modestly.

Jerry seemed lost in thought as he returned to where Leonard was
seated. He sat beside him on the stool and said, 'Lenny, you never told
me you had such a beautiful mother…'

Leonard looked up from the score he was poring over with perplexity and said, 'Beautiful? Well, I suppose she is, but you know, Jerry, you
generally don't lump your mother in with other women, I mean women
you find attractive in an aesthetic sense. Is your mother beautiful?'

'Well…um…I suppose she… Yeah, I see what you mean…'

Amid the ensuing silence, he suddenly realised that his mother was
in fact very beautiful. Despite all the hardship and abuse she'd suffered,
she had retained a physical radiance men would find appealing, all the
more alluring for the warm and generous character she'd managed to
retain in the face of adversity and which immediately drew you to her.
It was funny but he'd never noticed it before.

Leonard and Jerry sat at the kitchen table studying scores over a cup
of tea.

Jerry was distracted and kept getting up to help Leonard's mother
as she did chores in the kitchen. 'Here, let me get that for you,' he said,

stretching over her, feeling her body against his, as he brought down a heavy pot from an elevated cupboard. In the end, he stopped going back and forth from the table and remained by her drying dishes as she washed up.

Leonard sat absorbed in a score at the table. He went to say something to Jerry and noticed him by the sink chatting to his mother. 'Hey, what are you doing there? I thought we were going to try and compose some variations on this piece,' he said.

'Yep, in a minute, just let me finish up here first,' Jerry replied before immediately returning to his conversation with his mother.

Leonard looked at the pair of them and noticed how keenly they attended each other as they animatedly discussed cooking, about which Jerry seemed to have more than a passing knowledge. His mother looked uncharacteristically chirpy and beamed for the considerate attention so rarely afforded her. Smiling radiantly, like he remembered her doing as a young woman, he saw, even more clearly then, just how beautiful she really was. He shook his head bemusedly and returned to his work.

From that moment on, his mother always asked after Jerry and seemed to visibly transfigure into another woman when she knew there was an imminent visit. But more remarkable than this attachment was the cordial relationship that evolved between Jerry and his father. His father too grew to like Jerry and when he was around seemed relieved to have someone who could release him from his domestic isolation. Unlike Leonard, who barely tolerated sport of any kind, Jerry had an interest and knowledge of horse racing, football and golf, all the sorts of activities his father followed with a passion. Horse racing in particular, which Leonard considered as incomprehensible as the profoundest mysticism, engrossed them in conversation no end. This relationship was cemented when Jerry gave his father a winning tip that ended, if briefly, his habitual losing streak and brought him in a tidy sum of money.

It was not unusual for Jerry to offer his father a hand in the garden for, as Leonard was perpetually surprised to discover about his multi-faceted friend, this was something too he knew about. At times, Jerry would ask his father what he wanted done and set about completing it, freeing him to catch up with his mates at the local.

On one occasion, after Jerry had pruned the roses, his father was even heard to mutter with resentful plaintiveness directed towards his family, 'He's the only one who gives a damn about me…'

'You go and enjoy yourself,' Jerry would say, 'and at closing time I'll come and pick you up.' This he duly did because by then Jerry had acquired himself a car.

At such times, Leonard would shake his head incredulously for the irresistible charm and magnetism of his remarkable friend, a friend who possessed such seductive qualities even someone as intractable as his father couldn't resist him.

His mind flashed back to the time Jerry and his mother nervously accosted him in the lounge room and something of the same apprehensive impulse registered in his stomach as it had then, though of course mitigated in intensity by time.

His mother sat on the single sofa and looked quite unable to settle herself. Jerry stood behind her with his hands on the back of the sofa and his head bent forward pensively.

'What's the matter? You two look like you've seen a ghost,' Leonard said.

'We have something to tell you and it's not easy…'

He sat puzzled in the enduring silence and waited with apprehension. 'Someone hasn't died, have they?' he asked fearfully.

'No…it's…it's nothing like that,' stammered Jerry.

'Quite the opposite,' his mother said as she twisted her body slightly and placed her hand over Jerry's.

'Well, what is it?'

'Your mother and I – June and I – are passionate about each other…'

Leonard sat dumbfounded, unable to know what to think or feel. 'Passionate?' he said inquisitively.

'Yes, Lenny. You're my best friend and I felt you had a right to know, as did June.'

'I suspect, it'd be easier if I didn't,' he mumbled.

'I – we – didn't want to feel like we were deceiving you.

'When you say "passionate", Jerry, do you mean like…have you… er?'

'In all senses of the term, Len…'

He rested the side of his face in his hand, looking askew at his mother, and stared at her with bafflement. He really didn't know what to say or how he should react.

'I'm sorry, Lenny, but the truth is I'm never so happy as when I'm with Jerry,' she said.

'So what are you going to do about it, Mum?'

'Everything will stay as it is and we'll just keep this as a private affair between us. Perhaps you might think that seedy but what else can a woman do? And I'm not going to abandon my children. Do you hate me for this, Lenny, or worse, feel disgust for me?'

As she waited for his response, she cast her eyes down with a tinge of shame, dreading how he might respond. The idea of his best friend and his mother as a romantic couple just didn't seem natural and he felt uncomfortable. As he looked at her tense face, he recollected all the years of misery she'd endured and how, since meeting Jerry, she had blossomed into a woman who had started to feel beautiful again and had even reclaimed something of the self-respect his father's cruelty had beaten out of her. At that moment, the need for his approval, like she was almost seeking his permission, struck him as a painfully dangerous sign of the submissiveness still smouldering beneath the emergence of the welcome change their liaison had brought about. Any obstruction on his part might threaten the fragile belief in herself she'd rediscovered and bring about a relapse into her former hopelessness. His heart ached for her and he didn't want to stand in her way. So what if his mother and best friend desired each other? She had a right to happiness like anyone else. Didn't she? Surely she deserved that. Since this relationship gave her what she needed, then that was a good thing as far as he was concerned… Otherwise, what did she have to look forward to? What could be more soul-destroying than being condemned to living with a stinking drunkard like his father, who didn't give a damn what she felt and without the faintest hope of her receiving what any human being needed, tenderness and love?

'You don't need my blessing but thanks for telling me. Personally, I think it's wonderful that two people I care about deeply love each other…' he said, casting aside any misgivings he had.

His mother's taut face softened with relief and she embraced him, planting kisses effusively over his cheek while he smiled and hugged her reassuringly.

From that day on, they had entered a conspiratorial alliance in which they would work together to ensure his mother and Jerry could spend time together. When he didn't pretend to take her out with him, as he often did and to which his father couldn't object, only to drop her off at Jerry's place, Jerry would visit his home, at which point he would discreetly exit to leave them alone.

Today had been different because before withdrawing he'd been overpowered by the dying ambience of the space that contained the personal remnants he was leaving behind and in which significant memories had imposed themselves on him. It was almost as if they poured into him from the mysterious shadows gathered in its corners, shadows growing thicker each moment as the room seemed to slip farther into encroaching darkness.

He turned his head and saw a partial contour of his favourite seashell on the bedside table and remembered that glorious day on the beach. He saw his mother cuddling his younger brother as she carelessly smiled on the shore, making funny faces and childish sounds to keep him entertained. And then he heard his father call, waving him over from the rock pools he was investigating. When he got to him, his father produced a shell and showed it to him. It glistened with iridescent brilliance and they both stood amazed by its beauty. He had never seen anything so beautiful and longed to have it. His father saw the fascination for it in his eyes and, running his hand affectionately over his wet hair, gave it to him. Then they went with their prize and sat on the sand

and made sandcastles, trying to build a magnificent structure worthy of this perfect shell, which they surmounted on their construction as the crowning ornament of their shared labours.

In the midst of what seemed the fading sound of waves and seagulls screeching overhead, he saw, as he came back to himself, the ever receding image of his father at a time when he could still play and smile, a time before his youthful dreams lay in tatters about him, before he was broken with backbreaking toil and ravaged by alcohol, and when he had belief in a future, in himself, and an intimacy still existed between them.

He heard the subdued moaning next door grow louder with passionate intensity and his eyes moistened. He started to snigger involuntarily and, trying to control himself, bit into his hand pressed tightly against his mouth. Soon Jerry would be ready to go out and pick up his father, who would be slumped over the bar at the local pub in a drunken stupor. Barely able to endure the sound of the robust athleticism emanating from next door, he lingered on the image of his prostrate and pathetic father and, remembering his self-pitying affirmation that Jerry was the only one who gave a damn about him, winced with a suppressed titter. Then, from the tandem play of the voices he was trying to ignore, he heard his mother's rising pitch of breathless excitement above the deeper moans that accompanied it until both voices gasped in unison and exploded in a peal of ecstatic sighs. At the height of their crescendo, Leonard broke down in a fit of laughter. With his body convulsing, snorting uncontrollably and verging on what would have sounded at times like wounded shrieks had he not checked them, he turned over and clasped the pillow between his elbows, buried his face and smothered any sound that might escape him, stopping his ears and shuddering hysterically as tears of neither mirth nor sorrow, but perhaps something akin to both, fell on his pillow and were, as was each audible token of suppressed emotion, given to the erasure of its fabric.

Dimblewit

This story will appear as fanciful fiction to all but the most accepting of readers but it is in all respects a faithful account. I can understand how anyone could have serious reservations about the veracity of a tale in which the simple expression of a non-existent word could spur such unlikely and life-altering consequences for the persons involved but here it is as it happened.

My name is Terry. I'm a man in his forties who teaches English and in his spare time tries his hand at creative writing. I have never been published and may never be but, nonetheless, live with language as my *raison d'être* and even when I'm not writing, I am single-mindedly thinking about it, much as one might imagine a psychopath obsessively plotting his next sensational crime in all its lurid minutiae. Whether this compulsion of mine ultimately proves me to be a misguided nonentity living a completely ill-adapted and illusory existence or one who is actually fortunate because he has, at least, a passion for something to dedicate his illusory existence to despite the fact that he will never be published, the fact remains that but for a few friends I love I have little else to live for.

Now I don't know if it's a writer's trait, but I can tell you I'm a dreamer, constantly fantasising about the possible scenarios that present themselves in the most mundane situations, trailing off into realms of sheer improbability. Whether this whimsy is something of a predisposition that has drawn me to the art of writing as a means of accommodating my dreamy nature, or because, being a writer, I then necessarily, scientifically, have to direct my gaze away from the merely contingent details of any 'here and now' in search of some unfathomed or phantasmal significance perhaps only I can discover and plot, and which would justify a lifetime's deportment of relative futility, remains the ambiguous long and short of it on which I can offer no definite opinion.

Let me tell you, my socially active wife had for quite some time before the commencement of the events that are to follow not really appreciated my abstracted nature, or my tendency to dissociate myself from what was happening around me and wander off in search of a solitary nook to indulge my daydreams. She had, frankly, become very impatient with me over the years, so that I often found myself wondering if we still had anything in common. I rather thought, a little sadly at times, it was probably more a mutual dependence born of extended familiarity and no longer an evolving relationship that still bound us.

It was at one of my wife's soirees that this odd tale began. She was in conversation with my only real friend, Jarrod, and his wife Vera. I have known Jarrod since we were schoolkids and have the warmest regard for him. One could call him eccentric on account of the esoteric subjects he is naturally drawn to, from extrasensory perception to the occult arts. Were one to ask him why a practising psychologist would concern himself with such dubious subjects, he would most probably respond that since all such phenomena are expressions of the human spirit, they are no less important to understand, or at least objectively examine, than the obscurest problems of physics, the mysteries of religion or, indeed, the paradoxical minefield of sexuality.

Jarrod has an unfortunate tendency to mispronounce words, a sort of malaproprism but maybe something else besides. So, intelligent and sensible as he no doubt is, someone unacquainted with him might in conversation be thrown off the line of argument he is articulating and focus on a mispronunciation, mistakenly judging him to be uneducated, or even pretentious, rather than deflecting that distraction and thereby appreciating the 'thoughtful eloquence' of his perfectly lucid discourse. This oral defect, which amused his interlocutors, annoyed him no end. If he caught himself making a mistake, and often he didn't because his excited mind would be racing ahead to the next point, he would stop, mentally go over the word and carefully drawl it syllabically. This took him some effort and one couldn't but feel a sympathetic twinge on his behalf. By the time he had done this, those whose interest hadn't subsided in amusement stood by in uncertain anticipation of where his account was headed as Jarrod, embarrassed by yet another linguistic faux pas, awkwardly laboured to regain his train of thought.

As Jarrod spoke to my wife, Joan, I could see she was latching on to his every word with entranced affection, evincing him an admiring smile whose attractive charm I hadn't observed in years, well, certainly not with one cast in my direction at any rate. She really looked quite pretty again in that attitude. At one point, I noticed Vera stealing glances at me during this conversation, as if she were eager to engage me about something but as I had started to slip into one of my familiar reveries, it was a peripheral awareness, as was what Jarrod excitedly spoke about. It concerned something to do with an ancient mystical philosophy which had become the rage in Hollywood. Apparently, some pop star, Belladonna the exotic virgin or something – I wasn't paying attention and may have misheard it – had championed this philosophy. As is the case these days, when celebrities endorse something, everyone gets on the bandwagon and Jarrod was expressing his psychological interest in this phenomenon.

As my mind was focused on a literary problem I had been brooding over and which, for all its seeming significance at the time, I can in no wise remember now, it was then, in the midst of this conversation, that I inadvertently – innocently – let slip the word, or rather the non-word, I subsequently rued had ever passed my lips.

Jarrod had just announced the name of this trendy philosophy as 'the holy cabana', when I said, 'Dimblewit…' audibly to myself. I didn't know why I said that word or what, if anything, it meant. In the indeterminate moment between Jarrod's mispronunciation of Kabbalah and my utterance or, perhaps, a fraction of a second after that, it's hard to say, there had been a wry twitter whose enunciation jolted me from my absorption and directed my glance to a guest named Eddy, a professor of philosophy, who'd been quietly hovering within earshot of our conversation.

At that moment, Jarrod, Vera and Joan abruptly curtailed their conversation with something of a metaphoric if not audible collective gasp and fixed their widened eyes on me. Joan's expression was something of a scowl, Jarrod's one of offence or perhaps even horror and Vera's one of disbelieving surprise.

'What?' I asked in bewilderment.

In the ensuing silence, Jarrod's eyes transitioned from a momentary squint of severity to a downcast plaintiveness. The lower of his frowning lips quivered with emotion and seemed to suggest he was deeply wounded in some inexplicable way.

Joan exhaled petulantly, cast me a poisonous glance, and said, 'Come on, Vera, I need some fresh air!'

Vera began to follow but hesitated as if she were about to reach out to me with an almost entreating gesture but then recollected herself and departed.

After some moments, Jarrod looked up and muttered sulkily, 'You know, I didn't appreciate your comment.'

'What comment?'

'Calling me a dimwit in front of everyone when I mispronounced Kabb-al-ah. It was humiliating, particularly when Eddy laughed,' he replied.

'I said no such thing, Jarrod!'

'That's what I heard.'

'Actually, I said "dimblewit"…'

'Oh, so that makes it better, does it? I thought you were my friend, one of the few people I can be myself around without having to be ashamed of my occasional linguistic eccsimplicities.'

'But Jarrod, I wasn't thinking of you at all. It just slipped out because my mind was on something troubling me. In fact, I think it's got to do with a story I'm trying to nut out. It might even point to a solution in some weird way… I don't even know what it means…'

'Well, it's clear to me it's a pejorative term of some kind. And speaking of innocent slips, you have heard of those Freudian ones, haven't you?'

I retracted defensively at the stern cast of his eye and attempted to mollify the situation with levity by saying, 'Yes, a Freudian slip is a kind of linguistic negligee we all see through.'

'Hmm,' he grunted unmoved, 'if that witticism is your idea of a defence, then you've really just confirmed what I thought.'

'What's that supposed to mean?'

'That precisely because you weren't in a position to censor yourself, you let slip your secret hospitility towards me, betraying what you really think and, like your feeble joke, I all too clearly see through it!'

'My hos-pit… hostility towards you? Jarrod, come on!'

'See, you're doing it again – making fun of my missedpronounciation!'

I was finding it difficult to keep a straight face amid this run of errors Jarrod was making, no doubt because he was stressed, and for which reason I didn't want to make his predicament any harder. At the same time, I felt seriously troubled by the whole turn of events. I started to fear that I might break out into uncontrollable laughter, like one does when another's exaggerated emotional state, say of anger, evokes an equally hysterical sense of powerlessness in oneself, so that one is overwhelmed by an unbearable fusion of unwarranted ridiculousness and trepidation at one's plight. The torture of this state is compounded by the awareness that any such outbreak would only exacerbate the misunderstanding and make an already absurdly uncomfortable situation even worse.

In order to break the spell, I instinctively said the first thing that came to me, which was perhaps somewhat blunt, but just what was needed to redirect the current in which I felt myself being swept by before it took hold. 'You know, Jarrod, since you brought up Freud, let me say in my defence, consider this alternative. It's you who ascribed this non-existent word as a slight on yourself. My so-called slight might be nothing of the sort but really just the interpretation of someone who is overly defensive about a certain idiosyncrasy he has…an inferiority complex about it, to use the terms of your trade…'

Thankfully, the plausibility of this counter argument couched in a language he understood seemed to jolt him from his wounded sensitivity and the hurt look on his face subsided as he reflectively composed himself in consideration of what I had retorted. 'Well, as you say, that is a matter of interpolation, but the inferiority complex is actually an Adlerian concept!' he said curtly with face-saving one-upmanship before departing off in search of Vera and Joan.

I was upset that Jarrod had taken this non-existent word as an insult directed at him. It's not my habit to wound the few friends I have and I started to dread that given his sensitivity about his tendency to 'missedpronounciation', he might brood over this misunderstanding to the point where it would get completely out of hand and erode our friendship. These flare-ups between intimates usually have an unspoken history of festering resentment in the background. Perhaps I had somehow offended him on some other occasion for which this instance provided an opportunity for a roundabout redress? I hoped that wasn't the case.

I needed to be alone, to calm down and get my thoughts straight. Besides, as the party was taking care of itself, I wanted to look over the story I had been working on to see if this word, dimblewit, bore any relation to the text, or rather, the literary cul-de-sac I had painted myself into and which, looking back, may have been what I was dwelling on when it imposed itself on me. But first I went to the kitchen to get a beer to take back to my study. My head was buried in the fridge while I rummaged around looking for one when a voice addressed me from behind.

I turned round to see Joan. Though her face was one of dignified decorum in her capacity as hostess, I knew her well enough to sense the anger seething beneath its dissembled composure. She swept a glance at the guests in the lounge room and shut the kitchen door behind her.

Then, trembling with indignation, she approached me. 'You have

to spoil the little fun I have in my joyless existence as your wife – don't
you!'

'Huh?'

'You could see I was enjoying myself with Jarrod and you just had
to lay the boots in.'

'But…'

'Just because he takes me seriously, listens to me, has some regard
for me…'

'But what…'

'You needed to humiliate me in front of everyone.'

'But…but…'

'Oh yes, our darling Mr know-all unpublished writer can't even let
his wife make a simple point without having to show her up 'cause he's
so much smarter than she is, isn't he? Oh, God forbid she might have
anything useful to say for herself.'

'Joan, stop! What are you talking about?' I pitched my voice in perplexed frustration.

'Don't pretend you don't know! We all saw you hovering there with
that typically aloof superiority of yours and when I responded to Jarrod,
I heard you calling me a dimwit under your breath.'

'Oh no, not that again. Not you too.'

'Don't you give me that…' she launched aggressively before she registered what I'd said, halted in mid-sentence and asked, 'What do you
mean "not you too"?'

'Well, firstly, I said dimblewit, not dimwit, which is, as far as I'm
aware, not even a word, and secondly, according to Jarrod it was meant
for him, so you'll just have to get in line and wait your turn if you want
to claim it for yourself.'

'You can twist it round whichever way you like but I know what
you meant!'

'*I* don't even know what I meant!' I said, throwing up my arms in
bemused defeat.

'There you go again, see, belittle me if you like, don't take me seriously, be flippant. But let me tell you, it's one thing to get no consideration from you in our private life, I've come to expect that, but when you maliciously insult me in public that's another thing.!'

'I'm not being flippant and I didn't insult you in public. I didn't even hear you make a comment, for God's sake. I'm telling you, my mind was somewhere else and that word, whatever it means, was not directed at anyone in particular.'

'Then perhaps we're all dimwits in your infallible estimation – ha? As for your mind, it's always somewhere else. That's the problem with you! You're never in the same space as anyone else – certainly not me. Not that I'd bother any more but what would you say if I asked your opinion about this new dress I'm wearing which, of course you haven't noticed, or my hair, huh? Assuming you'd heard me, no doubt something indifferent like, "Oh, that's nice…" Then you'd bury your head in a book or walk off like I wasn't there. Nice! Ugh! I hate that nothing word from nothing people who have nothing to say.' she hissed shuddering with rage. 'Complete and utter uninterest in anything to do with me or what I care about, that's all I get from you. All you want to do, all you can do, is indulge in your useless mental masturbations. Well, no more, I've had it – you hear? As far as I'm concerned, you're a selfish, pathetic bastard and you can just –'

At this point, the door opened and Eddy peered in. 'Oh, I hope I'm not interrupting anything? Just come in for a drink.'

'No, Eddy, you're not – nothing at all,' Joan said with an uncanny blend of decorous contempt, the decorum in deference to Eddy and the contempt wholly reserved for me, as she exited.

Eddy looked at me with feigned nonchalance, probably to spare me embarrassment. It did the opposite because it meant he'd heard something of my flailing by Joan. He came in and, heading for the fridge, asked, 'Are you okay, mate?'

I didn't feel like speaking. In fact, my stomach was churning with unease. Joan's t outburst had really cut deep and I just wanted to disappear.

'Yes, Eddy, all good. Excuse me,' I replied as I made my way to the study, in the course of which I happened to see Jarrod and Joan looking at me askance from the corner of the lounge room, where they were huddled in fervid conversation.

I was really rattled and couldn't concentrate on anything. The idea of looking over any writing paled into insignificance as I sat in a daze at my desk. Nothing seemed to matter any more. I couldn't get my mind off Joan's tirade. Sure, we'd had our differences in the past but I'd never seen her so livid. She tended to be more the cold, distant type when she was particularly upset with me, as against her usual lukewarm impassivity when things were normal, but never like I'd just witnessed.

Having lost my appetite for anything literary, I considered just lying down in the darkness on the couch, closing my eyes and drifting off into blissful oblivion when there was a gentle rap on the door. That was the last thing I needed right then and I quietly sighed before responding, 'Yes, come in.' I sat with my head in my hands.

The door creaked open and Vera said as she poked her head in, 'I hope I'm not disturbing you.'

I waved her in without looking up.

She stepped in gingerly and stood with her back to the door behind me. 'Are you working?'

'Vera, I don't give a damn if I never read or write another word again. I'm fed up with it all.'

'But Terry, no, how could you say that?' she gasped as she drew a little closer. 'I love your stories. They're so entertaining and full of insight… I feel you understand women when I read them, at least a woman like me…'

I couldn't exactly guess what Vera meant by that comment because I didn't feel I understood her any better than any other woman. My general experience on that score has always been limited. We knew each other well enough, I guess, but I didn't feel we had much in common. She was at least ten years younger than the rest of us, thirty-four or so, and of an athletic bent, her active pursuit of fitness clearly visible in her well-toned and perfectly proportioned physique. In fact, coupled with her exquisite face, she was what was commonly referred to as a bombshell, and though I had at times admired her charms from a discreet distance, as any man susceptible to feminine beauty might, it was not with inordinate lust.

'Thanks, Vera…' I said flatly, releasing a defeated exhalation of self-contempt through my nostrils.

'It's true, Terry, you're brilliant! I love the one about… and that one where…'

Here she recounted tale after tale I had written and forgotten about with a precision of detail and occasional comment of insightful interpretation I found surprising. I didn't realise I'd shown her so many of them in the past.

I lifted my head and looked around at her with flattered bewilderment. Where she stood, beyond the reach of my small desk lamp, her figure hovered indistinctly. She stopped speaking, relaxed and drew nearer so that the obscured features of her face emerged in clear, if muted, relief in the pale light.

I went to gesture to her to sit down, when I winced with a sharp twinge in my neck.

'What's wrong? Oh I see,' she pre-empted before I could respond. 'Look at you, hunched over like that. I can virtually see the tension in your shoulders. Here, let me massage them for you. Now, don't resist. My personal trainer does this for me all the time and it'll do you the world of good.' She set about kneading my shoulders.

'Ow, easy there!' I cried.

'Goodness, I can feel the knots of tension in your muscles. You're in a bad way, my friend. You know, my personal trainer says that the tension in our muscles isn't only due to physical strain. It can have an emotional basis too. "Armouring", she calls it.'

'Armour-owing? How's that? Ouch!'

'Sorry, Terry, you'll have to put up with a bit of discomfort but trust me. Ever notice how people stoop when they're stressed? It's like they have the weight of the world on their shoulders and it's buckling them down. They're at odds with the world or maybe even themselves. It's like they're trying to protect themselves, fold back into themselves from the outer world, a bit like a snail shrinking in its shell,' she giggled, 'and if they don't pay attention to what their body is telling them, sooner or later they might crack – just like a snail – under the strain of what's burdening them.'

Thinking about my current plight as Vera spoke, I saw what she said made a lot of sense. All I had wanted until a moment ago was to collapse and disappear but her skilful attention was apparently mitigating that sense of darkness along with my physical discomfort. Feeling more relaxed with her as she worked my shoulders, I asked, 'So, enlighten me, Vera, in what sense do I understand a woman like you?'

'Well, you said it openly yourself, just before.'

'Did I? I don't recall…when?'

'When Jarrod, Joan, you and I were speaking in the lounge room.'

'I'm puzzled. What did I say then?'

'Well, at one point when Jarrod was speaking, I broke in with a comment which went unnoticed by the others because Joan just happened to say something at the same time but you heard it, didn't you?'

'No, not really, but maybe I've just forgotten. Tell me.'

'I know what I said was irrelevant, even foolish, and you were right when you called me a dimwit. I deserved it.'

I tensed up when I heard that onerous word that wouldn't cease dogging me!

'Hey, what's wrong? Relax, Terry. Don't give in to that armouring!'

Was there any point in telling her she'd misheard the word and misconstrued its meaning? Probably not, so I said in a throwaway manner, 'Look, Vera, if I said that, forgive me, it was unintended.'

'Spare yourself. No need to fib for my sake. I am a dimwit.'

Well, this was a novel turn, actually getting affirmation instead of condemnation for the misheard word.

'Vera, how can you, arrrh…you got the spot there… How can…

ooh, ow, there too, definitely got it there… How can you say that about yourself?'

'Because it's true. I'm just a body, a bare skeleton, that's all…'

'That's an odd thing to say. Looking at your healthy and, if I may say so, voluptuous figure, you're hardly skeletal.'

'That's what I mean, though. I'm nothing more than that, and that's all people see. I have no soul, Terry… I could feel most of the men in that room looking at me before. I get it all the time. I have to wonder how many of them would betray their partners if I was in the least bit interested in being seduced, and I'm not saying that out of vanity, I certainly hope not anyway.'

'I can't disagree with you there, Vera. I – er – noticed there was – um – general interest paid by those respectfully monogamous men in your direction. But um, I'm still not really convinced that makes you a dimwit, nor how that ties in with my understanding a woman like you.'

'Well, when I said what I did about those guys just now, you know, leering, there was at least one there who wasn't impressed by me at all, never has been actually…'

I had really started to loosen up under her delightful touch and was letting myself go in blissful relief, half-unaware of what she was saying and not really caring. 'Hm, that's good, ooh, ah…aw…'

'Do you know who that might be?' she asked.

'Hm, yes, yes, ooh, ah…aw…'

'You do!'

'Huh?'

'Know who!'

'Oh, no, I don't, but what's it matter?' I replied indifferently.

'You, Terry, you're that guy, and calling me a dimwit confirmed it. Hey, don't seize up again, let yourself go!'

'Now hang on, Vera, wait a minute!' I twisted around towards her as I sought to correct what I took to be a troubling misperception.

'Don't struggle, you'll ruin the effect, we're nearly there.'

'Okay, okay but…hey, easy there!'

'Let me explain. I don't mean anything to you, so you don't flatter me to try and bed me. That sits well with me. What a relief to be honestly appraised a dimwit than manipulatively put on a pedestal. That's the way with guys like that and, I admit, it often works. Women, I mean most women, have to take their share of the blame because they can't resist a good flatterer. On the other hand, despite the tactlessness of blatant flattery, one can't deny the simple convenience of the blunt approach if you're drunk and just looking for a quick lay without having to beat around the bush, you know? You appreciate that as a woman at times 'cause it cuts out the crap of pretending there's anything more to it than just sex. Not me, though, I hate that sort of thing. I want sincerity, just pure and brutal sincerity, so please, say it again, only not under your breath but forcefully this time – with passion!'

'Say what?'

'Dimwit…'

'Dimwit?' I repeated loudly with surprise.

'Oh, that word,' she sighed, her fingers picking up in pace.

'Yelp!' I cried as her fingers burrowed into what felt like a raw nerve. I turned my head from side to side in horrified bemusement, watching them as they pawed me like the talons of a cat in blissful abandon.

'Oh,' she huskily intoned.

'Ouch!' I duly replied.

'Mm…' she moaned.

'Oo-eee!' I writhed.

'Hold still! I, I…' she gasped, 'I so treasure your indifference towards me! That really gets me and all I'm good for. Jarrod, he's too kind, considerate, not at all what I need at times. I don't want to be doted on. I…excuse me for boring you, I know you're not in the least bit interested in what I have to say but that's just it, you see? It's your indifference, your unapproachable distance because you've got so many more important things to think about than someone as insignificant as me that…well…er…'

'I don't think your boring me at the moment is as quite an indifferent a matter as you think!' I said with tight-lipped irony as I felt her fingers gouging into sensitive crevices I never knew were there. 'Yikes, that hurt! Please get it over and done with!' I pleaded.

'It's, it's your total uninterest in me that's so…ooh…exciting!' she shuddered.

There was by this stage something of an involuntary and noticeable disturbance happening beneath my waistline that I was less than valiantly struggling against. I felt overwhelmed by delicious sensations of pleasure, in between the occasional jolts of pain in my upper body, and laboured half-heartedly for a means to free myself from Vera's clutches without offending her. While I couldn't help feeling there was something improper in my physiological response to her manipulations, I put it down to inexperience and told myself it was, perhaps, nothing more than the perfectly appropriate effect of a properly executed massage.

She sensed this tension in me and with something of an ambiguously rueful satisfaction ceased massaging, crouched beside me and said, 'I'm offensive to you, aren't I?'

'Let's not jump to conclusions, Vera…'

'Don't lie to me! I'm just a big bore…'

'Well, I wouldn't say…'

'I don't care. I can't help it. Chastise me if you must but…' Here she smacked hers lips to mine while emitting fugitive phrases in between a barrage of kisses. 'Tell me I'm useless,' she pleaded.

'Well, yourrr…' my response was smothered beneath her lips.

My head was in a whirl. Maybe it was the effect of the massage or just because I was getting some long overdue tenderness – sheer healthy animal contact – from a woman in such a long time, and that immediately after the roasting I'd just had from Joan, I don't know, but I couldn't resist and before I knew what was happening, I surrendered to Vera's assault.

'I'm still waiting,' she broke off, cupping my head in her hands, eyeing me expectantly in between slapping a torrent of kisses over my breathless face.

'Vera, if being useless makes you happy, yes, you're useless…' I said, gasping for air in that brief pause before she resumed pressing her lips to mine.

'And superficial,' she said.

'Yes, profoundly so…'

'Oh, that so turns me on! Don't stop!'

'Well…' I garbled '…you're the most shallow, unattractive dimwit I've ever met!'

Here she lost all reserve and pressed herself so forcefully against me that the chair I sat in leaned back, slipped backwards and crashed with me and her to the wooden floor! She continued devouring me as I struggled to recollect myself, my body pinned horizontally in the chair with the weight of her body pressed against mine as my legs dangled helplessly over the edge of the seat. I was done. I had literally fallen for her and gasped whatever sweet – derogatory – nothings I could think of to please her…

I don't think there's any point going into details. Anyone sufficiently imaginative might glean where things led to from there. I will only say that, yes, while I felt pleased by what had ensued, at the same time I couldn't help feeling dissatisfied with myself, particularly when I thought what Joan might think if she found out about this episode. Really, I shouldn't care, any more than I felt she cared for what I thought, but yet I did. Why was that?

My immediate answer was that though her attitude towards me was one of frequent severity, I did nonetheless respect her and would in no wise wilfully seek to hurt her. Yes, that was one possible answer. Another, though, and perhaps more plausible, particularly as I resisted admitting it to myself before an inner struggle, was fear, pure and simple fear – of her. Hers was the stronger personality and I shuddered to think what lacerating barrage of distemper she would hurl at me if she found out.

I let things go for some months, during which Vera and I would meet to indulge our mutual passion. This was no problem because Joan was frequently engaged with her own pusuits, though I must say, more so than was usual during that time. On the other hand, convenient as that was, I knew the situation couldn't go on. One way or the other, I would have to bite the bullet and own up to Joan or break it off with Vera. I was leaning more to the former, which would ultimately mean distress, recriminations and upheaval; in any case, the way things stood was getting unforeseeably complicated, practically and emotionally.

In the first instance, Vera insisted on enlisting me into sexual exploits which were basically foreign to me. She would want herself tied to the four corners of the bed with fine satin bindings so that she lay splayed on her back like a human X. Then I would have to verbally belittle her while caressing her body with something soft like a feather duster, intermittently flipping it about and running the rod over her skin menacingly until she was aroused to shuddering intensity. Seeing her excited, and responding to that excitement, I would ready myself to make love to her, upon which she would berate herself for her disgusting desires, declaiming she was unworthy of my attention and deserved to be left in a state of unsatisfied torment, at once resisting her climactic release as she thrashed ineffectually to free herself while goading me with crude solicitations to impose my will upon her. After having teasingly caressed her first with a firm hand and then a probing tongue before I mounted her, she no doubt relishing every moment of it, I drew uneasy pleasure in my symbolic role of a violator.

But the complications that troubled me increased because, even in that relatively brief span of time, the satin bindings quickly became coarse rope, much more to her liking, the feather duster a leather flail, and a perfectly luxuriant bed a hard, unyielding surface of some kind. Vera particularly relished the kitchen bench on and about which culinary instruments like knives, meat cleavers and the panoply of kitchen utensils arranged on magnetic racks heightened her excitement, almost as if they suggested something like the implements of a medieval torture chamber.

Her appetite was insatiable and, coupled with the specific accoutrements and *mise en scène* necessary to its satisfaction, exhausted me. I am a writer and live in my imagination, but frankly the exactitude of imagination demanded to fulfil her fantasies was becoming taxing.

One time, in a moment of inspired extemporisation, she leaned over the kitchen bench, handed me a wooden spoon and, lifting up her skirt and baring her buttocks, begged, 'Mon chef, get cookin'. Beat me – like an egg!'

While, in initiating this game, she wanted to feel as if she were the vulnerable one, the thought that Joan might walk in at any moment and discover us in what I considered to be a picture of ridiculous if not grotesque choreography, for which one could not possibly imagine the shadow of an excuse with which to exonerate oneself, it was actually I who was made to feel the vulnerable one. You know, I may have got away with that but I was never quite comfortable whenever I saw Joan using that wooden spoon afterwards, and it had to inevitably, mysteriously, disappear and be replaced by another.

The compounding complication during this time, if I may move on, was Joan's altered behaviour towards me. She had become quite considerate, even caring, so that I felt a nagging guilt when I recollected my betrayal of her. When I expected her to berate me for something, she, instead, showed unexpected tolerance. Whereas before she might not care if I fell asleep on the couch, so that I would wake up shivering with cold in the middle of the night, suddenly I woke up to find a blanket spread tenderly over me and a pillow tucked comfortably under my head. She no longer cut me short in mid-sentence with all-knowing superiority but listened patiently and considered what I had to say and, often, graciously agreed with my differing opinion. This was certainly puzzling and while I appreciated the civility shown towards me, at the same time I felt a resentment of the consideration rendered by someone who troubled my conscience for being the unwitting victim of a rotten deceiver like me! It really would have been much more tolerable if I could have justified a grudge of some kind towards her that would have put us on an equal footing, a kind of comparable moral flaw or mutual culpability, if you know what I mean, but, as that was not the case, her decency really quite upset me.

As one can see, I was a messed-up bundle of impulses shunting me uneasily between their respective objects, erotic and emotionally fulfilling, though socially reprehensible in relation to Vera, and, alternatively, conventionally acceptable though emotionally flat and sterile when it came to Joan, with me caught in the middle of this madness and at times feeling as though I were being torn apart.

One afternoon, Joan and Jarrod went to the art gallery to view an exhibition. Vera and I took the opportunity to meet at her place. The time got away from us because, unexpectedly, we heard Jarrod's car pull up the drive. There was, as one can imagine, a desperate flurry of activity to get ourselves into some kind of presentable order before he entered through the front door. I had managed to get my clothes on with stupendous rapidity such that Vera commanded in a panic that I go into the lounge room and sit down calmly as if I were waiting for her to buy time.

I heard Jarrod's key scratching in the lock as I sat on the couch and braced myself. When he entered, he looked at me with surprise as I flicked through a magazine that I had a moment before realised was upside down and managed, I think, to turn the right way up before he noticed.

'Hey, Terry, what are you doing here?'

Gulping nervously and taking a slow deep breath before emitting a stream of impromptu verbiage I had no control over, I replied, 'Look, I hope it's no bother, I don't mean to be a…bother, but there's a story I've written and er – I tried finding it, but can't – god damn it, that's annoying when you want to find something to get on with but can't – you know what I mean? Anyway, I think I gave a copy to Vera and was hoping she might have it. That's it, that's all there is to it…'

'Okay, okay, relax. Where's Vera?'

'She's in the bedroom. She was taking a nap. I'm afraid I caught her unawares and she's making herself decent.'

'At this time of day? That's strange. She's such a hyperactive sort. I for one can't ever keep up with her.'

I knew exactly what he meant and feared my attempt at subterfuge might have sounded a tad dubious.

'Jarrod, you're back, darling! Where's Joan?' she exclaimed as she entered the room sounding perfectly normal but looking uncharacteristically dishevelled.

'I dropped her off home. She's going to be wondering about you, Terry. She was expecting to see you there.'

'How was the exhibition?' Vera asked.

'The only way it could be with a painter like Monet – glorious. Hey, what have you been up to?' he asked as he looked at her attentively.

'Hmm, dear?' she replied with a look of wide-eyed ingenuousness.

'Your hair, it's all over the place.'

'Oh well – you know – I – er…' she fumbled for a response.

'The only time you look like that…' he said thoughtfully, at which I tensely bit my bottom lip… 'is when you've been having nightmares and you're thrashing about all over the place.'

'Oh yes…' she sighed with relief, as did I. 'You got it in one,' she affirmed.

Turning to me, he added, 'She keeps having dreams about being chased by someone with a weapon of some kind, she tells me. Wakes me up all hours of the night, she does. It's strange, when I ask her about them, she tells me she's terrified and yet the sighs, the moans she makes while she's dreaming don't sound anything like that at all. They sound more like…well…'

There was a peculiar look in his eye as he stopped short of what he was going to say, a sceptical one which put me on edge, like he was obliquely questioning her account and maybe by implication my excuse for being there at that moment, but that idea may have been nothing more than a consequence of my own guilt.

'Yes, dreams are crazy, aren't they?' I said stiffly, standing up in preparation to get the hell out of there as quickly as possible. 'Vera, did you find that story I was after about the unfaithful…about the faithless priest?'

'The faithless husband?' she intoned, cautiously looking at me for a cue.

'Priest!' I emphatically repeated. 'You know, the one where er…'

'He seduces the wife of…' she stupidly blundered in her attempt to lend a feigned recognition of the non-existent story.

'No,' I interjected desperately, 'the one where he's seduced by his best friend's – no, where he's seduced by what seems his most devout parishioner but who turns out to be an apostate from hell,' I said, wincing with embarrassment at the utter ridiculousness of what I was saying.

'Oh, that one…' she nodded as we exchanged knowing glances. 'That's what you were saying when I was half asleep before. Goodness gracious, I think I still must be. Sorry, I didn't quite get it.'

'Terry, do you want a drink?' Jarrod asked, creasing his brow tensely.

'No, Jarrod, I need to go as soon as I get this thing – must keep the creative juices flowing,' I said, subsequently ruing what an unfortunate turn of phrase that was given what Vera and I had just been engaged in.

'Well, I'm having one,' he said as he turned to the bar.

It was then that I noticed the slip Vera had hurriedly put on and loosely covered with her dressing gown had an awkward protrusion beneath the fabric over her right nipple where the front of her dressing gown splayed, just noticeable from where I was standing but, thankfully, not so obvious from the angle at which Jarrod had been in relation to her. I gasped.

Don't ask me why but one of Vera's crazes at that time was to have clothes pegs affixed to her nipples and, strange as that may in itself seem, she also enjoyed them strategically placed in sensitive areas of her nether parts. While Jarrod's back remained turned to us, I surreptitiously brushed my hand over her breast upon which there was a 'click' as the peg dislodged.

'Ow,' she yelped.

'What was that?' asked Jarrod as he cocked his ear in our direction while fixing himself a drink.

'Nothing,' said Vera, looking as if she had just remembered something. 'I'm just going to rummage around for that story of Terry's.'

She turned and making her way coolly to the lounge room door with what can only be described as superlative aplomb, I heard a further, 'click, click, click' followed by a muted 'ouch' as she exited.

Jarrod turned to me thoughtfully with a worried look. 'There's something serious we need to talk about,' he said as he swirled his Scotch in his glass reflectively.

'Oh yes?'

'Something that disturbs me…'

'Oh, what might that be, Jarrod?' my breaking voice emitted with suppressed dread.

'Something sensitive that concerns all of us but which is…er…not easy to broach.'

My heart sank.

After a long pause in which he stared at his Scotch, he uttered, 'But maybe now's not the best time for it… I don't know… Nevertheless,' he reconsidered as an afterthought, 'I must say, though, I'm not very happy about…'

Just then Vera came out with a stack of work I'd given her over the years and said, 'I can't find the exact one you're after but it's got to be among these. When you find it, please give the others back.'

'Thanks, Vera,' I said, relieved to have the pretext I needed to allow my escape.

'Among those?' Jarrod intoned quizzically. 'Shame you couldn't locate it, because I wouldn't mind having a look at it myself. It kind of struck a chord with me, or maybe even discord judging by the intriguing way you two seemed to be talking about different stories,' he said with a tone intended as humorous but tinged with something unintentionally melancholic.

'I must be going,' I said.

'But hey, what's that?' he exclaimed. He bent down and picked up the peg that had been dislodged from Vera's nipple, holding it up demonstratively as if he held a damning exhibit in some sensational legal proceeding. He creased his brow. 'That's funny, I keep finding these damn things strewn about the house lately,' he concluded with an interrogative turn of his head to Vera and me.

I wondered if he suspected the sinister meaning of those telltale pegs but couldn't be sure. I hoped to God Vera hadn't engaged in the same sort of sport with him but, you know, it never occurred to me to ask her.

'Ah-ha, I guess they must get caught on the clothes I bring off the line. You know how careless I can be…' Vera simpered innocently.

'Hmm…that explains it, I suppose. Terry,' he said, raising his eyebrow suspiciously, or maybe just curiously, 'do you realise both your shoelaces are undone? What's going on there?'

'Yes,' I said holding myself in check and wondering what I would say next. I feigned a wince of discomfort then said, 'These damn new shoes, Jarrod,' and fortunately they were, 'they pinch my feet something shocking. Whenever I get a chance, I have to loosen them! It's such a relief. Anyway, I'd better get going,' I concluded as I laboured to balance the stack of paperwork Vera had dumped in my hands.

'Don't you think you'd better tie them up before you leave? You might trip.' said Jarrod.

'No…ah, no worries, mate, what's a Freudian trip between friends?' I blurted stupidly, balancing the stack of useless literature in my arms, lamenting the lame attempt at a joke I'd just made out of nervousness while his wife stood there in her slip and whose utterance was really a betrayal of the fear he might be seeing through our charade as I prepared to skedaddle out of there.

He automatically smirked back at my witticism before his face assumed a stony seriousness in which his inquisitive eyes burrowed into me with an enigmatic stare.

My heart thumped as I made my way out of the door to the car,

'He knows,' I thought. 'He knows and was just toying with us – oh God, what a mess!'

The following week I felt sick, really sick. I couldn't muster the energy to do anything. I hardly ate for my distress. I was almost certain Jarrod knew of my cheating with his wife, and I knew too something had to be done immediately. It was better if I initiated the difficult task of admitting the unpalatable reality of things than if its admission were forced on me. There would be some semblance of moral collateral in that, at least. Previously, I had wondered what my wife would think about my infidelity, but why, I asked myself then, had I never seriously considered the feelings of my dear friend Jarrod? Why? I didn't want to hurt him! Was I secretly laughing at him in a way like he'd ascribed to me in the dimblewit episode? At the time, I had thought that mistaken, but who was mistaken, he or I? Was I only now thinking of my obligation towards him because of the prickly problem that I might have been caught out and not because of the innate reprehensibility of my actions, which is to say, because I was now adding moral cowardice to hypocrisy?

'That's the way with us humans,' I thought. 'We wound those we most love. We take their love for granted, treat it cavalierly until we're forced to confront the abuse of that love, that trust, only dreading the consequences when we realise there may be no way to retrieve what we've perversely trampled in the mud.'

At the same time, the convenient, and welcome, counter-thought arose. 'But how can you hurt someone if you assume, in fact, he doesn't know you're deceiving him?' That was, unfortunately, a fleetingly reassuring response because there arose immediately after the annoying counter to that counter-thought, 'Of course you're hurting him. Because your insincerity is foremost in your mind every time you're with him, you're inhibited by that, holding yourself back from him and, therefore, depriving him the unfettered generosity that makes for true friendship – your very self.'

That struck me as an odd thought beyond my capacity to assess in any clearly logical sense at that moment, a perhaps over-subtle and unjustifiable notion coloured by my emotionally turbulent condition. Whatever the case, one thing was sure, there was no getting round what a rotten skunk I felt.

At the first opportunity, I told Vera of my intention to come clean. She grimaced with trepidation at the suggestion. She felt it would destroy a sensitive man like Jarrod if he knew about our affair and in her undiminished love for him would prefer to spare him any pain. Given his tender nature, she seriously feared it would be an overwhelming double shock for him to discover that not only the woman he idolised but also his best friend had betrayed him. A further obstacle for her was what any admission would mean for us. She loved me too and, though it was in an altogether different way, no less intensely. It seemed that she could allow herself to be free with me in ways she couldn't with him and the prospect of having to sacrifice that was also painful to her; a gentle and romantic spirit like his could never be party to the type of risqué fantasies she needed to indulge and their removal would make that aspect of her life an unfulfilled emotional limbo. And then there was Joan: what would she think, I dreaded as I mulled over Vera's doubts. Just when she had altered her behaviour towards me for the better, there was I about to let a cat loose among the pigeons. Whatever the consequences, though, I could see no other way. The question then became a matter of timing, of picking the best opportunity as soon as it presented itself.

It wasn't long after I'd made up my mind that Jarrod invited Joan and me to his place. It was, ostensibly, to be a gathering like any other but I couldn't help feeling that the curt way he'd delivered his invitation presaged something dreadful I preferred not to think about. Whenever I did, my stomach churned uneasily with anxiety. I consoled myself that he would surely confront the situation of my philandering with his wife as I had imagined I would, intimately and one on one, and not in a public context; or, more likely, he would confront Vera first, upon which she would tell me and I would be prepared for the consequences, and that had not happened. That set my mind at ease because the remoteness of the scenarios I dreaded suggested no imminent disaster and hence no nasty surprises. Then again, I fretted quietly after these troubled consolations whether, perhaps, Jarrod might not want to shame me.

After the night of the dimblewit episode, I sensed at times he had become reserved towards me. Maybe he harboured a grudge and relished the idea of avenging the humiliation he believed he'd suffered publicly by embarrassing me in an equally public way before the witnesses of that event. That would be poetic justice, wouldn't it? If that were the case, I wondered what his intentions to his beloved Vera might be, vengeful or otherwise, but, whatever they were, I surmised they were probably of secondary importance to him. In his eyes, it was me, his long-standing friend, who'd proved to be his big-mouthed ridiculer and betrayer! He was wrong in that judgement, at least in significant part, but right or wrong, I couldn't stop him from thinking that way.

From the moment Joan and I entered the house, I felt uncomfortable, stifled by Jarrod's manner. I tried telling myself it was just me ascribing thoughts and emotions to him from my own sense of insecurity but the palpable sense of his restless stiffness was unmistakable. He had a bearing of formality uncharacteristic between close friends, or perhaps precisely characteristic, when a difficult problem impacting on their friendship must be broached and there is an inner conflict in oneself between what needs to be done and, for the distaste of it, what one would prefer to pass over. Except for moments when it was absolutely necessary, he avoided eye contact with me, as I did with him. Clearly, he was fortifying himself, avoiding any friendly exchange of glances that might mollify his resolve for the moment when he must make a move and denounce me with unmitigated prejudice.

Despite my initial uneasiness, however, I managed to collect myself, settle in and relax, making the occasional witticism as we all engaged in harmless small talk. Perhaps things were not as I had imagined, I consoled myself.

This sense of security abruptly ended when Vera asked Jarrod, 'When's Eddie coming? He should have been here by now.'

I was jolted out of complacency and back into my former trepidation. 'Eddie,' I thought to myself, 'was the other party privy to Jarrod's humiliation that night! He took particular exception to that philosopher's snigger when he mispronounced kabbalah. So that is his game after all,' I thought. 'He's going to make a meal of me in front of my wife and the rest of them! Hmm…'

'Why's Eddie coming? You didn't say so when you invited us,' I said, straining to keep my irritation in check.

'Why shouldn't he come? He's a friend of ours, isn't he?' asked Jarrod. Then lowering his eyes, he continued, 'But the truth is there is some business between us I need to attend to. He should have been here some time ago,' he said with an inconvenienced sniffle in concert with a fleeting curl of his top lip.

'Yes, business, of course,' I hissed barely able to disguise the sarcasm in my voice.

This didn't go unnoticed and I sensed the party ruffle uncomfortably with surprise at the unexpectedness of it, particularly Joan, who cast me a puzzled look.

In my state of growing agitation, I added, 'I suppose you've got something important to tell him along with the rest of us.'

Jarrod froze, taken aback, and fondled his glass clumsily with downcast eyes as he struggled to respond. He composed himself and said resolutely, 'Well, actually, yes I do…'

Joan leaned over to me and whispered, 'Terry, what's up with you?'

'I thought this was meant to be a social gathering,' I bristled.

'It is it is…of course it is!' Jarrod responded, looking disoriented.

I had to admit that the ingenuous look of surprise he managed in response to my challenge was quite a nice touch, very convincing.

Nonetheless, I got up and prepared to go, saying, 'Maybe we can hear what you have to say some other time. I'm not feeling well and don't want to spoil the party.'

'No! Wait, don't go just yet. What I have to say won't take long,' he exclaimed with an uncharacteristically commanding tone, stretching out his arm authoritatively to stay me.

'What about Eddie, then? I'm not waiting for him to turn up when-ever.'

'Don't worry about Eddie. I'll get round to that later.'

'I bet you will,' I muttered under my breath.

Compelled by the determined look he cast me, I slowly sat back on the sofa. There was a prolonged silence in which I fretted over what was to come. No doubt he was going to savour my torture by letting me stew in my juices as long as possible. Joan looked at him expectantly and Vera with what appeared to be curiosity. Apparently then, she wasn't privy to what would ensue; she certainly didn't seem edgy at all, not at least until I had spoken up petulantly a moment ago.

I'm the sort of person who has a nervous disposition, I'll admit that. I can easily fall into states of anxiety for what others might generally consider trivial or improbable reasons. When in those states I will often suffer in silence for months without anyone suspecting it in the least. There is, however, a definite tipping point at which some other side of myself seems to change gear and goaded by a kind of self-preservative revulsion at my deplorable condition – the constant sense of entrap-ment and vexation I endure – snaps and inwardly decries, 'Oh damn it, what I fear might happen can't possibly be as intolerable as being stuck in this pitiable state of avoidance of it, let be what must be,' upon which a relative calm creeps over me and I am emboldened to face what I fear. I had reached that tipping point and was prepared to run reck-lessly headlong into what may be in store, be it total disaster.

'Come on then, Jarrod, speak up!' I commanded.

Jarrod paced thoughtfully some moments, stopped, faced me and pursed his lips reflectively a number of times, almost like a man exer-cising his mouth, limbering it up like an athlete as he prepares to grap-ple with the difficulty of the task he is about to undertake.

'Well?' I said.

Sighing noticeably, he started, 'Okay, look…' at which point Joan got up to hand him a drink. He went to reach for it but then awkwardly halted with bemusement as he looked at the drink in his hand and the one she proffered. Joan flushed with embarrassment, grimaced submissively and sat back down looking distinctly uncomfortable.

'Let's just get down to it without any further interruptions or delay,' I said through my gritted teeth while uplifting an open palm towards Joan as if to say, 'You just sit down and be quiet.'

Responding to this gesture, she placed the glass in her curled hands obediently on her lap and averted her eyes from mine.

'Yes, yes…' said Jarrod. 'What I have to say is not easy…is…hard…'

'As I imagine it will be for all of us,' I interjected.

It was then I noticed Vera shifting uneasily in her seat. Only then had she understood the reason for my defensive acerbity and that there was, perhaps, more to this soiree than had initially been apparent to her.

A troubled look flickered over Jarrod's face and, visibly making an effort to compose himself, he responded to my comment with, 'Yes, that may be… In any case, Terry, I want you to know whatever may come between us, I have always loved you like a brother. I would never willingly hurt you, as I know you would not me…'

This sentiment, unquestionably true, cut me to the quick when I considered my betrayal of him and really hurt me more than any viciousness he could overtly exact in revenge. After all, something in me had already wounded itself in its duplicity towards him, and it was precisely that unbearable part of myself I wished could be cast off that resonated in painful sympathy to what he said. If this generous approach of his was the way he was going to cut me down to size, then I stood no chance and could only acquiesce to the inevitable conclusion that I was, indeed, the lowest of the low. Nonetheless, this show of generosity irritated me. I didn't want to feel trapped submissively before his humility, a clever ploy, I felt, to keep me on the defensive but which my survival instinct to prevail, my selfishness if you prefer, refused to submit to without a fight.

'Sometimes, most often, we don't live up to our ideals and it's always easier to see the failings of others than ourselves but we must be generous, accept change, life is change and er…what's a good example?' he asked himself fumblingly. 'I know, it's like this. However much we want to hold on to our youth, for example, we nonetheless have to accept change and age gratefully, if you see what I mean.'

'No, not really. But, whatever you're getting at, I think you meant "age gracefully",' I responded.

'Hm… yes, age gracefully…that's right.'

'And?'

He cleared his throat, trying to gather his thoughts after my correction. 'My point is simply…er…life, you know, throws up all sorts of challenges along the way and well, quite frankly, one is often not ready for them, one quite often fails, dismally, but one must…er…adapt, accept those realities even when one is shocked, shocked and mortified not only by them, those things, bad enough as they are, but, even worse, the way one chooses to deal with them, the poor way one tackles them and which always comes down to just – for better or worse – oneself,' he ended with a strained show of conviction after his somewhat diffident address.

I thought it extremely clever the way he was attempting to put me at ease, using a conciliatory tone that would induce me to lower my guard as he primed himself to pounce and checkmate me unawares; his apparently hesitant, diffident, address was one of masterful guile one couldn't but help admire. He had read me astutely. I was mortified by my actions, I loathed myself because of them, and this seemingly conciliatory approach was the best way for him to get maximum emotional leverage over me, striking right where I was most vulnerable and didn't want to face – my shame; yes, that was the case but nonetheless I wouldn't give in and couldn't help retaliating, 'When you say "one", Jarrod, do you mean me, you or anyone?'

'Well, all of them, of course!'

'Oh, really? That simplifies matters. So we're talking about you, me and everyone then?'

'Now, now, Terry, don't split hairs… Why so peevish? Please, don't make this harder for me than it already is…'

'And you don't think it's just as hard for me?'

Jarrod retracted with a kind of fearful recognition, as if what he felt was his secret bombshell to divulge had somehow already been exposed and compromised so that he seemed to wilt with the shock of it. Joan and Vera too succumbed uncomfortably to the growing tension in the room.

'Look, Terry, it's like this: basically, you're my friend, there's a bond, an allegiance between us that…er…I feel has been betrayed and I don't like it, want it, you hear?' he pitched his voice dissonantly such that we inwardly reeled at the unexpected force of it, including Jarrod himself, apparently to his own surprise.

I would have to be careful because this was a passionate, explosive side of Jarrod I'd never witnessed before.

'And you, Vera,' he continued forcefully, 'have been the love of my life, the one and only whom I've held in the highest esteem and put on a pediment…'

'Pedestal,' I said irritably.

'Yes,' he agreed with a look of annoyance, 'you'll have to excuse what one might term my occasional speech impedestal…'

'Impediment,' I couldn't help pitching in sadistically.

'Im-ped,' he began reiterating carefully before Joan exclaimed, 'Terry, must you? Just let him speak for God's sake!' She said this with a tone reminiscent of her former irritability towards me that she immediately checked with the flicker of a deferential smile in mid-sentence when she became aware of it.

'Go on, Jarrod,' she said encouragingly.

'Where was I?' he asked himself.

'The love of your wife!' I misquoted sarcastically, upon which Joan cast me a disapproving glance.

'Did I say that? Hmm, I meant the love of my life. I'm sure I said "my life",' he reflected as he thrust his jaw out nervously to loosen his neck from the clinging of his sweat-soaked collar. 'Anyway, Vera, you know I love you and I know that at times I haven't lived up to giving you all the detention you thoroughly crave – the at-tention you deserve,' he corrected himself. 'I hope you don't blame me for that because whatever's happened I never intended any disneglect…'

Joan shot out a preemptive look of prohibition at me to keep my peace.

Jarrod's face glistened with perspiration. Great beads of sweat clung to his forehead and apparently stung his eyes as they rolled down his face, for he needed to brush them away with his equally sweaty palm a number of times.

As he sniffled nervously, I wondered if perhaps what he wiped from his eyes was not only the sweat from his brow but even incipient tears. In fact, it seemed as if he might be in a state of inner, if outwardly composed, distress.

He drained the whisky he had in hand in an apparent attempt to steel his resolve and continued, 'Hmm, look I'm rambling and will cut to the chase.' Here, he fumbled around in his pockets and pulled out a crumpled handkerchief with which he wiped his face before saying, 'Looking at the two of you, my best friend and my wife, I have to say before you here and now with the utmost humidity that I'm quite sad, disappointed, and have at times even felt disgusted –'

So here it was – the knockout blow I knew was coming. In the brief moment in which these words were spoken, but which seemed to linger for a torturous eternity, I noticed Vera fidgeting in her seat uncomfortably while her toes, visible through her slip-on sandals, retracted tightly as though struggling to grip the ground she felt about to give way beneath her. She averted her eyes from Jarrod, put her hand to her mouth remorsefully and held her breath. I rolled my eyes up as if supplicating some merciful higher power to spare me the torture of the moment, a funny instinctive gesture for one who believed in nothing other than himself and therefore had nothing else to appeal to or blame for the lamentable pass to which things had come.

'– disgusted that something as sacred as friendship, our friendship, should be abused and betrayed by those we trust. Oh, how much the worse our pain when wounded by those we love! Oh Lord, that I know. And so I say to you both, Vera and Terry –'

My hackles were up! Though I had no justification for it, I was about to lunge at him with a host of excuses, extenuations and even denials when the imputation of infidelity irrevocably left his lips.

'– I want to ask you in all humidity, on behalf of myself and the woman I love, Joan, to forgive us for our having been ungrateful to… accuse me I meant… exc-use me I meant un-faith-ful in friendship to you. We have no excuse except the sincere and irresistible love we have for each other…indeed, have hopelessly fallen prey to…'

My body had already begun to preemptively lurch forward with the index finger of my right hand in the act of thrusting forward aggressively to meet the oncoming assault when I froze in mid-flight, holding that finger extended in perplexity.

'Huh?' I barely muttered to myself dumbfounded.

'I'm sorry, Terry and Vera, truly. I beg you, can you find it in your hearts to accept this difficult situation and maybe even forgive us? We have suffered much for it.'

As I sat there dazed trying to make sense of what I'd just heard, I could see Joan looking at me askance with dread, poor Jarrod standing before me like a condemned man hoping against all hope for a last-minute reprieve and Vera agog with disbelief.

The sudden combination of a staying of the disaster I had expected, the release of the tension that had kept me on a knife edge, along with my complete misreading of the situation and the grotesque irony of Jarrod's and Joan's parallel infidelity, for which they were imploring a forgiveness I too had secretly yearned, all came together to overwhelm me so that I collapsed into a fit of hysterical laughter. Like a madman, I guffawed and bellowed with abandon, unable to control myself, slapping my stomach and shrieking discordantly the harder I struggled to rein it in.

They stood by in bewilderment, looking at me solicitously, and perhaps imagining the horror of Jarrod's disclosure had unhinged me, the thought of which, along with the way they gravely exchanged glances at each other, only succeeded in provoking a continuance of the comical convulsions which were by then making my diaphragm ache.

In their concern for my condition, they crept up to me with the intent of rendering whatever aid they could but the look of troubled seriousness on their faces only redoubled the painful laughter I dearly wished would stop.

'Are you okay, mate?' asked Jarrod

In between gasping for air and clasping my abdomen painfully, I waved them away.

'I told you, didn't I, perhaps today wasn't the best time to tell him,' said Joan.

Jarrod nodded worriedly.

I waved them back to me to tell them there was no cause for alarm. I inhaled deeply in readiness to make the difficult effort to do so in one quick burst but could only manage, 'Oo! Ow! Hoo! Oo! Ow! Hoo!' as another wave of belly-splitting laughter ensued. I shooed them away again. These unsuccessful attempts at clarification that were attended by my beckoning and then dismissive gesticulations happened a number of times.

'Do you think we should call a doctor?' asked Joan.

'I don't know. Maybe. I've seen this sort of hysterical response in analysis when clients are confronted by something too painful to accept. I hope we haven't broken him,' replied Jarrod.

I waved my hands energetically to get them to desist from that idea but with my eyes dilated imploringly and my face contorted wildly as I struggled to make myself understood it really must have appeared that I was something of a madman in need of medical attention.

'What does he want?' asked Vera, as nonplussed as the others by my behaviour. 'One minute he waves us to him and then the next he shoos us away. Maybe we have to do something.'

I slapped the armrest of my couch three times in quick succession, shook my head prohibitively and then gestured with my open palm the need for a pause as I waited for that bout of laughter to pass.

Eventually, it subsided and a relative calm began to ensue.

I brushed away the tears of hilarity from my eyes and without looking at them forced out with difficulty, 'Don't worry about me and please wipe those distressed looks off your faces or I'll crack up again…' I started to chuckle with the memory of those solicitous expressions but managed to contain myself.

Still refusing to look them in the face for fear the incongruity of their concern with the reality of the situation might spur another fit of hilarity, I said, 'Relax, sit down. I have something to say…it's okay, there's nothing to worry about.'

I could feel the welcome ease of tension in the room as I came back to myself and they, in their bewildered way, did as I asked. Clasping my aching abdomen, I composed myself and prepared to speak. 'Firstly, Jarrod and Joan, if there's anything you think you should apologise for, it is, speaking for myself, accepted.'

I looked at Vera with a subtle flicker of my eyebrow to see whether I had licence to go on in the name of both of us. She understood and nodded.

I cleared my throat. 'I understand better than you think how something like your relationship could have happened. We all get ambushed by events. Secondly then, if there's anything to apologise for, I, along with Vera, extend our apologies to you both.'

Jarrod and Joan exchanged puzzled glances and trained their faces on me with curiosity.

'I also understand what you've been going through and it's admirable, truly, that you had the courage and decency to come out with it in your sincerity. The basic fact is, Vera and I have developed feelings for each other and let's just say we have been no less dishonourable to you than you feel you were to us. It was my intention to speak up too but, well, whether out of fearful procrastination or lack of opportunity, I failed where you succeeded.

'But there's another thing, Jarrod, I'm ashamed of, more than anything. I'm sorry that I misjudged you. I had suspicions you knew about our affair and wanted revenge. I don't want to harp on a situation I know was painful to you, but I convinced myself you were resentful of me for letting slip that ridiculous word dimblewit which you took personally that night at my place, and that, maybe, you were lusting for some payback for the humiliation you felt I'd cruelly inflicted on you, a lust I feared compounded by your knowledge that I was cheating with your wife. That was very ungenerous of me to malign your character like that, as if you could ever be so spiteful – I see that more than ever now – and if anyone stands in need of exoneration for anything, it's me.'

Jarrod sat quietly down on the sofa beside me. We all sat there in stunned silence with our heads bowed. Jarrod looked up at Vera, who was sitting diagonally across from where he was seated, and she looked back at him. After a moment, I did the same to Joan, she being in a corresponding manner sitting diagonally across from me, to which she responded, our four gazes intersecting at some imaginary point between us. In a strangely synchronous moment, we all bowed our heads pensively and remained so for a spell.

Jarrod stirred, cleared his throat and said, 'Terry, we're all prone to bouts of shadow boxing at times. I did take that inadvertent word as a slight. I was furious, but you were right when you pointed out it was really a matter of misinterpretation. I suppose it came hot on the heels of my "cabana" slip and Eddy's chuckle really cut. He's such an intellect whom I admire and I was mortified. This idiosynchrony of mine – hold it a moment, pol-y-sy-ll-ab-ic words are especially tricky – this id-i-o-syn-cra-sy of mine is something that has dogged me all my life. You can imagine the putdowns and mockery I had to endure in the schoolyard. Actually, you know it all too well, Terry, because you were there, and you always proved a true friend who shielded me against that cruelty. Well, that never leaves you, that old anxiety about being judged a fool or laughed at.

'Being a psychologist should make one wiser but it in no way makes one immune to one's basic blind spots. We are, after all, only human. I should have known better, Terry. You would never have purposely set out to wound me. So there, don't be hard on yourself. I was in my own way just as ungenerous.'

'Thanks, Jarrod, that means a lot to me,' I couldn't help responding.

'But, you know,' he continued, 'I'm glad it all happened the way it did because without that silly non-word, Joan and I might have never discovered our love for each other.'

'How's that?' I couldn't help asking.

We were all by this time freely communicating and looking at each other without inhibition.

'As I said, I was furious at you and so was Joan –'

'Terry, I'm sorry, I really am!' Joan interjected, leaning forward towards me in her seat with a look of genuine consideration for my feelings I hadn't been privy to in years.

I nodded with an absolving smile.

'Well, we were really hacking into you. As Joan thought that supposed insult was meant for her, she was really prickly too, I mean really! Looking back, initially there was an almost comical tug o' war between us over whom that jibe belonged to! We split the difference and claimed an equal share of your villainy. Well, didn't we suddenly have something in common to get passionate about! So, in our mutual distress, united by a common enema, sorry en-em-y, as it were, we forgot ourselves in our support for each other. Funny, from our wounded self-absorption, we were suddenly consoling each other, affirming how perverse your supposed judgement was, whomever it was intended for, and what wonderful people we thought each other to be. So words of consolation became supportive caresses and that was followed by a moment of unspoken recognition – you know, that electric flash between gazes where something invisible in one's self collides with something invisible in another and which you both feel – simultaneously!

'Our anger dissolved and we were transported by an uncanny passion, so sudden, in which everything else dropped away as unimportant.

Now, I'm guessing our feelings for each other were probably always lying dormant – Joan and I have always been close – but those feelings never seemed anything more than platonic and certainly would never have blossomed like they did if that odd series of circumstances had never arisen.'

We were startled by a loud knock on the door. Vera went out and returned with Eddy, who was intoxicated.

'Hello, all! Sssorry I'm late but I got sss-sss-sssidetracked,' he slurred.

'You got sozzled, that's what you got! Where have you been?' asked Jarrod.

'Esscuse me…hmm?' he began as if about to respond but stopped in perplexity. He staggered over to Jarrod and thrust his quizzical face to him, eyeballing him intently. 'Do I know you?' he asked, swaying on his feet.

'Eddy, don't be silly, it's me, Jarrod.'

'Are you sure?'

'Maybe you'd better sit down.'

'How do I know which one to believe? There're two of you there,' he quipped, patting Jarrod on the shoulder with bonhomie as he lurched from side to side.

Vera went to assist him but he held out his hand for her to desist.

'What happened, to answer your question, is I double-booked, and its gone that way all day, double, double, bloody double – everything double. I even threw up twice,' he said, waving his hand. 'Let me ess-plain. I, that's me, and sss-some of my colleagues, esssteemed philos-soph…esteemed phosophorousosophers…oh fuck it, thinkers,' he hicupped, 'had a pre-Christmas drink.'

'Eddy, Christmas is well over a month away,' said Jarrod.

'Ss-so? It'll be on us ss-sooner than you can sssay Rip Van Winkle, Winkle, little star, how I wonder…' He started singing childishly while waving a metronomic index finger in accompaniment before ceasing abruptly with a vacant grimace and recollecting his train of thought. '… And one must be prepared for any opporimpunity to have sssome fun! Besides which, do we really need a festerive season as an esscuse before we can allow ourselves good sswill to all hamkind? No! Of course not!' he said emphatically with a rhetorical flourish of his arm whose sweep terminated in a raised index finger set before Jarrod's face. 'But it wasn't awll just fun 'n' games…it was er…what's your name again?'

'It's still Jarrod.'

'That's a funny name. How long have you had it?' he giggled. He waved his hands wildly as if to negate the need for a response and said, 'It was what one might call a ss-symphonium…sssymposium.'

'A symposium…what about?' asked Jarrod with a smirk.

'It was a sssymphonium on all the boutique beers that have sprung up in Victoria over the last twenty years. The range of 'em is virtually infinitesimal,' he said with a grand sweep of his arms as if to indicate an extensive quantity. 'One of my colleagues there couldn't believe his eyes…' he hiccupped '…but that's hardly surprising because he's a pro-fessional sssceptic,' he sniggered. 'In fact, I told that doubting Thomas there and then that like all ssseptical men of the séances, "He could dis-tinguish chalk from cheese, but always missed the wood for the trees." Yep, ssso help him, I did!'

'Well, Jarrod,' I said, 'I'm curious to know why you've called this intellectual superman over today.'

Scratching his temple amusedly, he said, 'I've been invited to a con-ference to give a paper on psychology and its philosophical foundations, its precursors and so forth. As I'm not really up with the classics, I was hoping Eddy here could offer some advice, perhaps point me in the right direction. I wanted to get that out of the way before you arrived'

'And he can,' interrupted Eddy, 'and he can, yes, Eddy can!' With an introductory hiccup, he added, 'Plato, now there was a ps-ss-ychologgical trailblazer! For incense, he proposed this piece of applied ps-ss-ychopoligymy for determining the characatures of the upcoming male generation: upon reaching puberty they should be made drunk on alcohol. Since *in vino veritas*, drunkenness would disclose their or-nate trendencies. Ssso, was one an ass-ss-ertive marshal type fit for the warrior class, for incense? Was one a deflective thinking type fit for the phosphorescent kingly class, or was one a matrealistic mercantile type sssuited to farming or partisanship? The booze would bring that out! One could then cultivate their native orientalations and channel them to their perspective porpoises. I, for essample, am living proof of this principle because when I drink I can't but become more thoughtful and, indeed, have made a vocation of that trendency…'

'Being thoughtful or drunk?' muttered Joan sarcastically.

Eddy didn't seem to hear her and continued. 'Ss-Seneca, Seneca, now there's another philosopholickle psychopollogist. Do you know he had to tutor Nero? Now, I ask you, really, who could handle having to mentor a nutcase like that and still keep a cool head, keep a head per se for as long as he managed, unless he was a truly great psychologist, hmm? And sss-ssspeaking of Nero and all that pychopathagynacology, do you know he had his mother murdered? Think of it! Evidently, no one esplained to him how the Oedipuss complex is supposed to work…' he concluded with a hiccup.

Vera resolved to be firmer with Eddy and, clasping him supportively said, 'Come on, Eddy, I think you'd better go to bed.'

He looked at her with studious interest. 'Are you a philospherer?' he asked.

'No,' she replied.

'Well, if that proposition of yours to go to bed isn't a philosophistical one, am I right in assuming it's my good fortune – it's a lewd one?'

Vera shook her head with a smirk and said, 'Come on, you need to lie down.'

'Done it again, I'm afraid, fallen for the phallus –' hiccup – 'fallacy of ambiguity… Still, a natural cause to that effect when one considers her a posteriori…' he mumbled to himself.

She had nearly managed to get him out of the room when he released himself from her grip and staggered to the middle of the lounge, upon which there was a collective sigh of sufferance for what other nonsense might follow.

'Before I go to bed with this young lady here, there is sssomething I need to bring up,' he said gravely, upon which he put a hand to his mouth and started to dry retch.

'Quick, quick, a bucket, something to shove under him!' cried Vera as we scurried about looking for something suitable.

I grabbed the first thing to hand and put a bowl of half-finished potato salad under his chin.

'No, not that!' cried Vera.

The look of the potato salad placed under his nose, which in Eddy's mind appeared at that moment not unlike the dislodged contents of a stomach, only succeeded in accentuating his discomfort and he turned away disgustedly with both hands frantically clasping his mouth.

Joan rushed back from the kitchen with a large, empty cooking pot and attempted to place it under Eddy's chin but in the midst of the tumult he'd created, his stomach had somehow managed to settle without incident but for a small deposit of saliva on his sleeve.

After a pause, he continued, 'I have held my peace too long!'

'Not long enough, unfortunately,' Joan muttered, shoving the pot on the table irritably.

'Ss-some time ago, oo-oh, peraps, I dunno know essactly, I was at the house of my very good friend what's-his-name here,' he said, pointing to me. 'And it pained me to see that man, as men of talent the world over so often are, not only misunderstood but vitrified. You there…' he said, pointing to Jarrod, 'were offended when he called you a dimblewit –'

'I didn't call him that!' I protested, concerned this fool might reopen the wounds we had amicably redressed to our collective benefit.

'It's okay, what's-your-name, let me do the talking. And so were you!' he pointed to Joan. 'Let me ss-slay empathically that you both misheard him. He didn't call you dimwits at all, though peraps he should have called you deaf…'

'How dare you!' bristled Joan, upon which Jarrod calmed her with a gesture of his hand and an indulgent glance at Eddy.

I buried my face in my hands and shook my head in dismay.

'Now him – that guy – is a man of letters who trucks with the creative poss-possil-possiliberties of language and it's not his fault if he sometimes ends up with words that don't in practuality persist. No, no, no! That's a preoccupational hazard. Fertility is the mother of all prevention…' He stopped, creased his brow, realising there was something awry about the supposed apothegm he thought he'd just uttered but then waved his hand dismissively.

'Anyway,' he continued, 'I researched what he said and it doesn't persist if you take it to be one word but does if you take it as two. Dimble wit is a perfectly ass-asseptiple combination of words. As a dimble is a deep and shady dell, or dingle, and a dell can mean a wooded hollow or a deep hole or pit, then it's clear to me that by metasporical esstention this good man was acknowledging the depth of your intercourse – a fact to which I believe you'd both agree – thereby affirming the perfectly profound sense you were making when he pronounced you, Jarrod, or you, Joan, or you both in conjugation as – dimble wits!' he said with his arms extended triumphantly in anticipation of the party's inevitable ovation for such a closely thought out and sensibly argued train of logic.

He lingered for some moments in that thoughtful attitude with something of the aura of an intellectual paragon or even perhaps world historical genius who'd taken a Gordian knot of contention hitherto confounding the greatest wits or statesmen of any age and who, in deftly untangling what ignorance and discord had set awry, decisively realigned the scales of universal apportionment back into balance for the good of all.

'Thanks, Eddy,' I said. 'I'm glad you cleared that up.'

'Yes, yes,' the others agreed.

'Thank you, it's nothing really,' he said, deeply moved and bowing graciously.

'Now come on,' Vera said, guiding him gently, 'off to bed.'

He waved her away with the misguided self-assurance of a drunken man who's convinced he's perfectly capable of deporting himself and began walking deliberately to the bedroom with his arms splayed out for balance, negotiating with each step what seemed an imaginary tightrope. He stopped, tottered momentarily until he felt comfortable of his reestablished poise and then, recommencing, suddenly lurched unexpectedly on a diagonal trot that only terminated when he smashed his shoulder against the lounge room doorway. The force of the impact made him whirl about and out into the hall, where he collided against the wall immediately opposite and from which he was heard ricocheting from one surface to another until his impromptu dervish ended in a cacophonous crash to the floor.

Vera ran out to attend him. We'd all instinctively risen off our seats to do the same but she called out to say there was no need for concern. We could hear her helping him up and knew for certain everything was all right when we heard her admonish, 'A-ah, Eddy, now you keep your hands to yourself!'

'It sounds like she might need some help,' said Joan as she exited.

Jarrod walked up to me and said wryly, 'I'm kinda sorry Eddy's had to go. You know, he made me feel pretty good about myself every time he opened up his mouth tonight. Nice to hear someone else making a complete balls up of it for a change – shame he's got to sober up.'

'Yeah, and such an intellectual giant too,' I smirked sympathetically.

He put his arm on my shoulder and looked at me tenderly, his eyes moist with emotion. Before we knew it, we were hugging each other, both tearfully relieved and grateful for where we had arrived or, rather, returned. He broke off, cleared his throat and excused himself for something he had to do. Painfully conscious of the worthiness of the man I had unjustly vilified and whose fragile humanity now struck me as something marvellous, sublimely inviolable, I watched him exit.

And so there it is! The characters of our tale – my very good friends – have left us and now there's only you and me. As I said at the outset, due to a misunderstanding (a non-existent word), things took a life-changing turn for the characters involved in this tale. Fortunately, that being so, things have worked out in a favourable way I could not have foreseen and for which I'm really quite relieved.

In fact, due to that word dimblewit – or phrase, dimble wit, if one looks at it Eddy's way – I was able to dispense with all the problems of the story I had been engaged on – the story that had been haunting me and to which you were never privy – when it first arose, affording me by its means the opportunity of supplanting that fraught attempt at storytelling with this alternative piece of writing. So then, the story told, I can let you go on to live your life in that curious world of yours I'll never fully comprehend while I, just another character amongst others, though for the purpose of this story one privileged to be the possessor of a narrating 'I', can now also retire with my fellows in this altogether different world of mine, a world which is somewhat of the stuff of an eternal present and which I dare say you too will never fully comprehend.

The Bookworm

'If I do not find something better to do soon, I shall grow pale and plump at my desk in a graveyard of old words.' – Meia Geddes*

From the time Gerald was a boy, he much preferred to read books than play games with his schoolmates and this unsociable tendency continued into his adulthood. Though he was extremely knowledgeable, he didn't feel he had much to say in ordinary conversation and always stood around, somewhat awkwardly, in the midst of those who rhapsodised over such things as beautiful homes, good food or that week's football matches. He was nonetheless a well-meaning man and out of politeness did his best to dissemble an interest in such things without letting on he really found all such inconsequential talk and its unreflective participants quite boring.

In his spare time, he relished nothing more than sitting down with a good book and the more avidly he consumed it, the more painfully aware did he become of the incomprehensible number of great literary works yet to be read. He was insatiable when it came to texts and even when he ate breakfast couldn't resist reading the nutritional information on a packet of serial and making mental notes of unfamiliar words or scientific terms he must follow up.

He had often reflected that were he to be marooned on a desert island, he would prefer ten of the greatest books ever written than ten living persons for company. Ten great books, he was wont to muse, would distil the finest qualities humanity had to offer, unlike actual

* From *Love Letters to the World*, Poetose Press, 2016

people, who were a bundle of incoherent and troubling contradictions. In his idle moments, he composed lists of what those books might be, which he'd constantly rearrange in a dizzying and inconclusive array of permutations. This task was all the more difficult because there were still so many reputedly great works he hadn't yet got around to. Based on the ones he had, though, he often thought that *The Complete Works of Edgar Allan Poe* would be a candidate, something of Dostoyevsky's, almost certainly Baudelaire, perhaps the Bible, more so because of its indisputable centrality to all Western literature than for any spiritual solace he might need on his island, Freud's *Interpretation of Dreams,* or Jung's *Symbols of Transformation,* or both, Frazer's *Golden Bough*, the complete edition, Chekhov's best short stories or Maupassant's, or both, Thomas Hardy's complete poetry and definitely Nietzsche's *Thus Spoke Zarathustra* to name but a few possibilities.

He would realise then, immediately after having chosen a book like *Thus Spoke Zarathustra*, that extraordinary book which he felt straddled and even somehow transcended the apparent divide between philosophy and poetry, not to mention something of the shadowy art of prophecy, in its audacious reorientation of the concerns of western culture, that that would necessitate he took the Bible along because without that book Nietzsche's work would make little sense. Deciding on that then, he would consider how he hoped to have some mastery of German and Hebrew before he found himself stranded on that island. Then, having apparently decided on these two definite choices, he would hesitate. Surely he would have to take something of Plato's along, otherwise that would exclude that other fertile current of Western culture so essential to an understanding of Nietzsche and all he strove to think against. Oh dear, he'd fret, he really should have something more than a passing acquaintance with ancient Greek, along with German and Hebrew, if he were going to get the best out of Plato... And so thus he would reflect, in an eternally recurring circle of reveries...

These thoughts were in this case no reverie but currently circulating in his head as he came to realise he was emerging from a state of unconsciousness into one of wakefulness. Once he had registered that thought, he further realised he must actually be awake but couldn't understand why, since he knew his eyes to be open, he couldn't see anything. Not only was he enveloped in complete darkness but, to his growing alarm, uncomfortably aware he had no idea where he was!

He reflexively spread his arms apart and found them obstructed by barriers on either side. Now completely terrified, he gasped as he considered the possibility he'd somehow been entombed alive! He was about to scream when he realised his body was actually vertical, if seated, and he could recall no occasion in his reading experience in which corpses were buried in a seated position. He cast his right arm out before him and it extended limply into empty space. It would be strange to be in a coffin, or tomb, not approximately spatially uniform in its envelopment of the corpse. Instinctively, with a forceful turn of his body leftward, he thrust his searching left arm back and it collided against the wall immediately behind him, twisting his thumb with the impact, the momentum of which forced his wrist to flick back and slam against it. He howled as much for the shock of unexpected obstruction as for the pain endured, which was really relatively mild. Nonetheless, he stuck his thumb in his mouth and sucked on it soothingly as his baffled mind ticked over his incomprehensible plight.

The proximity of the wall behind him got him wondering and he twisted his body round on its seat, this time to the right, to tactilely explore what was immediately present. In doing so, he realised that his legs seemed to be bound by some kind of material that made movement difficult, though not impossible. He felt along the wall behind him and his hands encountered what appeared to be a protrusion of some kind that felt like it was made of a plastic material. Twisting a little more, he ran his right hand along the projecting object, which was perfectly smooth, except for one area which he surmised to be at its middle, located at the line immediately adjacent to his body. His forefingers exerted the slightest pressure in their investigative probing and seemed to indicate that this rectangular facet was not as resistant as the rest of the material and even suggested considerable give. With irresistible curiosity and not a little trepidation, he pressed it and was surprised, or rather relieved, to discover with the gushing release of water that ensued that it was a flushing cistern.

Now he remembered where he was! He had been to a book launch and had drunk more of the free wine available than was his wont. On the way home, he had stopped at a library he'd just happened to encounter to kill two birds with one stone. Firstly, he could avail himself of the lavatory as his stomach was churning with discomfort, and after that he could take a look at Kafka's *Metamorphosis*, a story he'd read many years ago but which he wanted to revisit because it had come up as a reference in something else he was currently reading. He had clearly been in no fit condition for Kafka and must have passed out. So he was in the lavatory of the library and what he had thought were bindings over his legs must obviously be his trousers around his ankles. He checked to discover that that was the case. But why was everything dark? He looked at his wristwatch with its illuminated hands and numerals to discover he must have smashed it a moment ago when his hand had collided with the wall. Nonetheless, he could make out that it had stopped at 11.30 – p.m.! Much as he loved libraries, he felt a queasy sensation in his stomach even more distressing than that induced by alcohol when he realised he must have been somehow overlooked and locked inside one of them.

He fumbled around for some toilet paper, cleaned himself as best he could in the dark and hitched up his trousers. It was going to be no easy task finding his way out of the library. It was not a familiar suburb in which the launch had been held and this was not a library he knew. He wished he'd been more attentive to the layout but had been so desperate to get to the toilet he'd paid scant attention to anything but that need.

He unlocked the cubicle door after groping around for a bit and now had to decide which way to go, left or right, for he could not remember how he'd entered. Being right-handed, that was the direction his natural inclination induced him to investigate, besides which, he was still intermittently sucking the throbbing thumb on his left hand for whatever palliative respite that afforded.

He felt along the cubicles, one then another, and considered how vast what must be a relatively small space can seem in the dark, particularly without the aid of familiarity to yield one some memorial definition of it. The thumb and index finger of his sliding right hand eventually met an interfacing wall. He placed his palm flat against it and surmised he must have passed the final cubicle and that, as most enclosing walls do, come to one that sat at right angles to its related boundary. It was troubling that his hand hadn't noticed the point where the final cubicle door terminated, the groove that allowed it to turn on its hinges, so he retraced its motion until he detected it. He then went back to the newly discovered wall and, just to be certain, ran his finger vertically down the point of contiguity of what he took to be the right angle of two planes, while waving it from side to side to determine he had arrived at two adjoining surfaces, of which he was convinced.

What he had to do now was to see, assuming he had gone in the right direction, if he could locate a surface distinct from the wall that might prove to be a door. He would have to run his hand slowly on its leftward trajectory in order to detect anything like a groove between the wall and door, because the textural change of the differing materials, say wood as against plaster, might be so minute as to be undetectable with a careless sweep of it, as had just happened.

It is impossible to determine a true sense of time without light and what it makes measurable, visibly calculable motion, so he had no clear idea of its quantitative passing but he had been meticulously running his hand along the wall for what seemed an interminable span of it without remotely detecting anything like a door. He was now feeling quite anxious and thought that he must have chosen the wrong direction. He considered walking across to where he imagined the opposing wall and its door might be to truncate this oppressive interminability but knew from previous experiences of stumbling in the dark that one can very easily become hopelessly disoriented even in a familiar space.

Such a move might make things worse, much worse, than his current plight. He thought it best to just continue on his course, however long it took. As long as he had something as palpable as a boundary he could follow, logic told him he must traverse the gamut of its finite points until he reached his intended destination or, at worst, returned to his point of departure, which would be, at least, preferable in maintaining some sense of orientation than haphazardly stumbling in the dark.

He had made the sensible decision, for his hand met a third adjoining wall. He only hoped he hadn't somehow missed the door he was after but thought that unlikely given his slow and scrupulous progress. He continued moving leftward and bumped against something with his knee. He felt it and realised it was a standalone ceramic urinal. It appeared he was on the right track. He was able to pass rather efficiently over the two consecutive urinals and placed his right hand against the wall immediately before him after doing so. It was now just a matter of arriving at the next adjoining wall and he would have the surface that finally held the promise of his liberation.

He located it and, eager with the anticipation of his imminent release, carefully ran his hand along it. After some moments, however, his hand slid past its surface and continued over its edge into empty space. With the shock of this unexpected eventuality, he reflexively retracted his hand and placed it back on the surface immediately traversed, instinctively slapping it to reaffirm its palpability. Briefly disoriented with troubled bafflement as he did so, he realised to his relief that he must have simply arrived at a partition of some kind. He wrapped his hand around its edge and, locating its parallel surface, little more than a handspan in width from one edge to the other, followed it round until he arrived at the termination of the partition and its interfacing wall. He continued until he reached what must surely be the right angle of the third and fourth walls.

After another indefinite span of time running his hand carefully over it, he encountered the groove he was seeking. He ran his hand up and down the door to see if he could find a handle, but with no success.

For sake of thoroughness, before he moved on, he put the tip of his second, and longest, finger to the groove, kept his hand perpendicular to it and ran it slowly up and down to see if the base of his palm encountered anything like a light switch. Being unsuccessful, he estimated various distances away from the groove as best he could and repeated the action a number of times. He was fairly certain of his thoroughness and surmised the light switch must be located somewhere near the opposite side of the door. All he had to do now was run his hand across the door to its opposite groove and he should be able to find the handle and, one would assume, a light switch nearby. This he duly did. He switched it on and with the sound of the flickering neon couldn't restrain himself from exclaiming, 'Let there be light!'

Sighing with relief, he affirmed to himself that no finer collection of words had ever been written. He would definitely take the Bible along to his desert island with or without Nietzsche. Glancing at the washbasins to his left and the mirror above them in which he stood reflected in his erstwhile enclosure, he fell into one of his familiar reveries. He had never thought about the meaning of that mysterious sentence in any but the most literal, that is to say superficial manner. Something, call it God, had to first let light be while everything remained void and formless. Being as we know it could never ensure its own manifestation, it took light to allow that, and that light had to be emanated by something it could never, itself, make visible beyond it. Perhaps the Greeks never really got to such a subtle notion with their fascination for the primacy of form and matter, but then again, as he vaguely recalled, hadn't Plato said something to the effect that 'the Good' was beyond Being? He was halfway through telling himself he would have to follow up that thought when he came back to himself to realise that there were really more pressing matters to consider at that moment than abstruse philosophical speculations.

He opened the door and could see obliquely, across a narrow passage, what appeared to be the open expanse of the library. As he cautiously started crossing the passage, he noticed the toilet door automatically beginning to close behind him. He wanted to keep it open as much for a reference point, a beacon of sorts he could always look to for some orientation, as for the scant and inadequate light that spilled through the toilet into the immediate passage where he stood. He attempted to adjust the overhead pneumatic hinge to fix it in place but with no success. It would need something jammed against it but there was nothing of sufficient weight in the toilet. Perhaps he could sally forth, find some suitably voluminous tomes and stack them against it?

As he pondered over the difficulties of how he was going to find an exit, he considered that perhaps the best course of action would be to go and randomly select some books on the shelf closest to him, which he would still have to locate, take them back to the toilet and bide his time there until someone found him in the morning; after all, any attempt to force the doors, which he remembered were automatic sliding doors, would most probably set off an alarm. In one fell swoop, he would go from being a fool who got himself accidentally locked up in a library to a thief caught in the act of attempted burglary. The resultant lock-up would no doubt be even more unwelcome than his current plight; besides, it wouldn't be altogether unpleasant sitting there all night reading books, as long as they were the right sort.

He had no sooner considered this a real possibility than he felt a sickening feeling when he remembered that the following day was Good Friday. Nothing would be open and he would be stuck there till the following Tuesday! No amount of good books would compel him to endure such a condition however pertinent as practice it might prove for his desert island scenario. No, he would have to try to find a way out.

The toilet door had closed behind him during these reflections and he became aware that his eyes had adjusted to the darkness. From his vantage point, he was able to make out, however indistinctly, the shapes of racks of books and shadowy conglomerations of perhaps desks and chairs arranged here and there for users to occupy. All his life he had loved libraries more than anything but now, surveying the vague blocks of blackness before him, he could think of nothing more desolate and forbidding, nor could he help feeling that there was nothing quite so melancholic, eerie even, as a public space plunged into a combination of darkness and desertion.

It was fortunate that there was a full moon that night because that, along with whatever incidental light was passing through some of the unscreened windows from the street lights outside, did ameliorate what would otherwise be near total and unbearable darkness. With care, he could even negotiate his way around now he felt. Perhaps he could find the main desk, locate a phone and call the police to inform them of his plight. Whatever they might think, he assumed there was no risk of trouble in reporting what was nothing more than an unfortunate accident; surely, no punitive consequences would ensue for turning oneself in as the victim of an unintended eventuality, or, to put it bluntly in the terms they would most likely think of his predicament, no cause for censure in his registering a plea for help for an inadvertent if salient instance of stupidity.

Things were not as dire as they first looked, he consoled himself. It would make sense to see if he could find a phone. If he failed, he could rest assured he would find one in the morning so there was really nothing to worry about. He ventured out to see if he could find some object to stop the toilet door, a reasonably sized tome wedged between it and the doorframe would suffice to maintain an opening large enough to allow a shaft of detectable light to shine through. Perhaps any book would do but he couldn't help preferring one of the largest possible for maximum light. At the rack of books closest to him, he felt along its shelves for a book of optimum width. Something like a telephone directory would be perfect.

There was nothing he felt suitable in his vicinity and so he decided to walk between the shelves and run his hand along them. All he had to do was remember he'd turned right into them at his beginning and make a note of each turn. The next would obviously be a left into the next row and then a right and so on. If need be, he could simply reverse the directions and he would inevitably return to his toilet beacon. As he did so, however, he fell into a reverie. Marvelling at the collection of books, none of which he could clearly distinguish, he felt as though he were some minute being travelling between the furrows of a gigantic universal brain in which the sum of human knowledge could, in one way or another, be accessed. Each book was like an incalculable network of connections that could link up with any other and he, perhaps like a neuron, could be absorbed and passed on from one network to another just by opening any one of them and reading it, assuming sufficient light, of course.

When he came back to himself, he realised he'd got somewhat lost in his thoughts and hadn't been taking stock of his progress. He felt a fleeting moment of anxiety but assured himself all was well. As long as he remained among this group of racks, he just had to walk back and follow them along to get to his starting point, the number of racks traversed being of no consequence. With a feeling of relief, he decided to press on, when he stumbled over something which precipitated him headlong to the floor.

His chin hit the carpet and came to rest in a cold substance of some kind. It gave off a putrid scent and he pulled away in disgust. He wiped his chin to discover a foul ooze of a type he had never encountered. It had something of the viscous quality of oil but stickier and elastic in consistency like phlegm. He could feel a strand of it hanging from his chin. He pulled out his handkerchief and wiped it off, along with the matter on his hand. After doing so, he sniffed his hand and again detected a smell conducive to nausea. He reflexively put his handkerchief to his mouth with dry-retching revulsion but this only had the effect of making him sicker with the proximity of the odoriferous substance smeared on it. He thrust it aside petulantly, wiped his face in his sleeve, and sat with his back to the shelves as he attempted to recompose himself. He was baffled. What could such a substance be? Was there perhaps a leak of some kind, maybe in the roof? There was, after all, an extended downpour that day.

After some moments, he decided to go back the way he came and give himself a thorough scrub in the toilet. In his disgusted eagerness to get cleaned up, he forgot the obstruction that had been the cause of his accident and tripped over it again, this time, thankfully, landing on dry carpet. What is that damned thing, he thought with annoyance. He grubbed around to discover a circular metallic stool of the type used in libraries to aid access to the higher shelves. In his frustration, he hit the stool with his hand as he prepared to get up.

He thought he heard a subsequent sound of some kind in response to his blow. He hit the stool again and once more a sound responded. Could it be an echo? He thought not because, though he could not make out the nature of the sound, it seemed to have an altogether different quality. He did so again but this time there was no response. He stood up and strained for any sound but heard nothing – just unbroken and inconsolable silence. Maybe his nerves had got the better of him and he was hearing things?

He had perhaps become somewhat complacent and told himself he must be more careful as he proceeded to avoid any further accidents. About to recommence, again he heard something. It sounded like a rummaging of some kind. He wondered if it might be a rat or something of the sort. Immediately after thinking that, he heard the crash of a stack of books and, startled by its suddenness and volume, recoiled against the shelves with the thought that it would be a rather big rat that caused such a cacophony. He called out but received no reply despite that he could distinctly hear something moving about.

He was now feeling quite alarmed because he was sure that he was not alone and whoever – or whatever – was there sought to remain elusive. The toilet would be his best bet. If there were anything dangerous lurking about, he could barricade himself in one of the cubicles; but now he'd have to chance getting back there after having betrayed his presence. But surely, he wondered, trying to calm himself, he was just overwrought and missing some perfectly reasonable explanation.

There was another loud crash and he promptly concluded that this was possibly no time to be reasonable. Overcome by fear, he proceeded to retrace his steps as quietly as he could but in his heightened state of alertness became painfully aware of each conspicuous press of his foot betraying his presence with each creak of the carpet.

Eventually, he got back to the first rack and had to find his way through the passage and back to the toilet. He had managed the first task as far as he was able to determine and set about trying to find the door handle. As he swept his searching hand along the wall, he heard a sort of sniffling, gurgling sound behind him. He turned and thought he could detect something moving but couldn't make it out distinctly, and wondered, with inexplicable unease, if he would believe his eyes even if he could. Across the floor, at another series of racks, there appeared to be a spectral, elongated entity emerging from one of them. It had to be some trick of the eye, he told himself, but thought he could see it crawling between the racks, the undulating curves of its motion articulated by the shifting sheen of muted light falling from a nearby window. It stopped beside a rack and appeared to take an interest in the contents on one shelf. It twisted its vermicular body into an erectile column and ran it up and down the shelves, almost as if it were sniffing for something; that, at least, is how it seemed.

What he witnessed next was beyond comprehension. It started audibly chomping on the books it selected as desirable for consumption and, extraordinary as that itself was, accompanied this behaviour with a phenomenon no less astounding. While it greedily ingested the books before it, it glowed with a lurid and pulsing luminosity. This phenomenon made the thick, long follicles on its body grotesquely visible, as it did the workings of its inner organs and the distended, blue veins throbbing through its translucent, glistening length. As it only appeared to glow when it ingested books, he wondered if it had a metabolism so efficient, so ingenious, that their almost immediate digestion converted them into bursts of illumination.

After a spell of gluttonous consumption, it paused and emitted a curious sound. He pondered on how one might describe that peculiar emission and, after as much deliberation he could reasonably spare in his now distressed condition, came to the conclusion it might be characterised as a kind of long and satisfied belch. This state of satisfaction, however, did not last long and it presently began foraging for more food.

Stooping abjectly, wishing he were invisible, wanting nothing more than to locate the elusive door handle that might aid that wish as his hands frantically fumbled for it, he couldn't focus on his task, nor tear his eyes away from the terrible prodigy before them. It was now no longer glowing and appeared to have become quiescent but he soon saw its gargantuan silhouette lumber away from the shelves. In the next moment, it reared slightly, its rounded foreparts adumbrated by the light from the window at its rear as it began to sway from side to side, like he had seen leeches do when scenting their hosts, while making sniffing sounds in its attempt to locate something. It ceased wavering, fixed its attention in his direction and then descended with a heavy flop to the floor. Its amorphous form appeared to be in motion again and he could hear gurgling sounds which he took to signify the gastronomic contractions of a stimulated appetite growing distinctly louder.

In terror, he gave up trying to locate the door handle and ran for cover amid the bookshelves. He located his entry point with impeccable precision and wove between them with new-found facility in his attempt to put as much distance between himself and that…that…bookworm!

Driven by an instinct for survival that accelerated the speed of his thoughts and their sharpness in clarity, he only then registered that he'd sensed the pale glow of a nearby window at the place where he'd previously tripped. He would make for that window and see if he could somehow open it. After having had that thought, he recollected the stool that had hindered his progress and determined to avoid it. For that reason, he slowed down and started kicking his left foot out to test for any obstruction before taking the next step. Meanwhile, he could hear the snuffles and gurgles of the bookworm as it prowled about the racks in search of its next illuminating morsel.

It wasn't long before his foot met the nuisance stool with a hollow clank. He felt along its circumference with the tip of his shoe and placed the ankle of his left foot at its boundary furthest from the rack, upon which he swung around it with a feeling of satisfied accomplishment. He quickened his pace and had taken just a few steps when he found himself reeling backwards as a consequence of stepping into the slippery slime collected on the carpet, which he'd unfortunately failed to take into account. He came down heavily in the cold miasmic puddle and felt it soaking through his clothes. Once again, he became aware of its grossly offensive odour and struggled to find his footing as he wallowed ineffectually in the putrid matter until he was able – finally – to generate the necessary traction with which to extricate himself.

As he kneeled against the shelves, panting from his exertions, he could see a pale radiance emanating beyond the crisp, vertical silhouette of the end of the rack, and felt relieved that his memory had not deceived him. All the while, however, he could hear the now snorting and grunting crescendo of the bookworm as each of its vermicular undulations, homing in on their prey, seemed to work it up into what sounded like an orgiastic frenzy.

He burled on past the end of the rack and could see the welcome window aglow with moonlight. After a cursory glance, he determined there was no latch by which it could be opened. Turning round to face the end of the rack he'd just passed, he made out a number of copious volumes on the top shelf. He seized one and angling it to the window to catch the light saw that it was Kroner's *All-purpose Lexicon of Literary Terms*. That was a promising title, he thought. He held it firmly in his grip and, bracing himself, charged at the window with all the force he could summon, slamming the spine against it. This only succeeded in producing enough reactive force to make him spring back from the impact and fall back on his rump. Nonetheless, he got back onto his feet and pounded and pounded at the window with all his might to no avail. As he did so, he lamented over how something so bulky in matter as it was weighty in concepts could actually be so useless in achieving the simplest of practical tasks when one's life depended on it. As he kept hammering away, it really seemed to him, in a not altogether comprehensible mixture of metaphor and hysteria, that everything he ever believed in, everything he ever prized, had no real effect on a world that remained recalcitrant to it, and, almost as if to affirm this thought as he further descended into unbridled fear and panic, the book's spine broke as a result of his pounding and collapsed into a broken and limp artefact in his hands, through whose slimy grip it slipped and fell impotently to the floor.

He fell to his knees in his growing despair and wondered if he were going mad, blissfully mad, slipping into that merciful condition that enables one to nullify the terrors of exterior reality by an inscrutable logic of utter disassociation from it, perhaps just like the subtlest and most erudite forms of intellectuality. In any case, he must be going mad, he thought, and thank God for it, for then he could surrender himself to the absurdity of existence with no further responsibility for confronting it required of him.

A moment later, though, he realised, almost despondently, that the very fact he retained an ability to affirm the possibility of his diminishing lucidity more than likely meant he was as abjectly sane as ever and needed to get a grip on himself if he wasn't to end his days as just another glutinous deposit of slime on a library carpet. He looked around and could see no chair with which to assail the window after his first lamentable attempts and so turned his gaze again to the heavy tomes on the top shelf. He scurried over to grab one when he was intercepted by the looming and awe-inspiring vision of the bookworm rearing out of the shadows with a voracious growl as it prepared to lunge at him.

In the available light reflecting off its hideous features, he could see it had no discernible eyes by which to negotiate its way but did have two enormous slits for scenting which tremulously flared as they drew in the aroma of his presence in a long, continuous sniff. The whole of his arm could easily be accommodated in them; and its mouth, if one could call it that, was a ghastly abyss of hard gummy serrations dripping with putrid slime hanging over its edges and capable of desiccating something even as impenetrable as Joyce's *Finnegan's Wake,* vellum-bound, with one effortless incision of its jaw.

For the first time in his life, despite himself, he reacted with a feeling unadulterated by anything remotely like circumspect reticence and released one uninhibited shriek of terror in the face of the inexplicable reality before him. Turning away from that horrible vision, he bolted with a complete lack of habitual hesitancy at the window and, evincing an athleticism he never dreamt himself capable of, achieving a momentum sufficient to penetrate the intercepted medium, crashed through it and ran down the street howling like a madman.

Next morning, he awoke with a start to find himself ensconced in a corner of his lounge room, leaning uncomfortably into it. He vaguely remembered returning home, jittering with terror, and collapsing there. He wondered if he'd dreamt the whole thing but his persistent fear seemed to indicate that that was what he would prefer to believe and not the reality of things. He noticed then the shattered watch dial and looked at it – it was frozen at 11.30 – and his thumb had started to bruise at the base of its nail. With his body aching and sore with cramp, he struggled to stand and noticed, after having done so, the disgraceful state of his clothes. They were stained by something that had stiffened the fabric as it had dried. As his face was moist with perspiration, he went to pull out his handkerchief but, of course, found none. He always carried a handkerchief! Something was pinching his neck. He pulled his collar aside to seek out the irritant when he dislodged something and heard it hit the floor. He picked it up to find a fragment of glass! It was then he detected a faint scent whose offensive quality rising from the iridescent splotches on his clothes sickened him. He needed no further convincing and scurried off to the shower to wash away the physical traces of the night's ordeal.

People noticed that Gerald had discernibly changed. He had apparently lost his addiction to books and even acquired an aversion for anything mildly reminiscent of a repository where any number of them might be gathered. He had also become attached to people and avoided the solitude he once relished, seeking to remain in their company as long as possible, especially as the night approached. He also became quite garrulous, accosting anyone who might want to listen to his rather incoherent narratives.

His acquaintances were all quite amused by the sudden transformation of this man to whom they had formerly alluded as the 'bookworm', as much for his pale, shy demeanour and weak bespectacled eyes, as for his pension for remaining sequestered out of daylight and buried in a book. That, at least, was the initial reaction but the more they interacted with him, the more impatient, irritated or patronising they became, for, inevitably, he would bore them with the idiotic tale of a gigantic bookworm that inhabited a certain library. Referring to the accounts reported in the newspapers, the clippings of which he had kept and was prepared to show them, he would insist that the carnage wreaked on that library was not an act of vandalism but something of much more sinister import. Then, like Coleridge's ancient mariner, he would feel compelled to retell the whole ridiculous, tedious tale all over again.

He cut a lone and pathetic figure when his interlocutors responded condescendingly or revolved their index fingers at their temples behind his back. He was not unaware of these things but considered the relation of his story of greater importance than what people thought of him. Even so, he knew it was a big demand to expect people to believe a tale like his – indeed, he would have much preferred not to believe it himself. He might as well have tried to convince them he'd seen the Devil himself, for though he might adduce as evidence for such a dubious existence the fact that sinister things happen all the time, that there is unwarranted depravity and unnecessary evil offensive to all people who pride themselves on being members of a rational species yet who nonetheless periodically succumb to fits of collective mania as if in the grip of demonic possession, he knew no one seriously gave credence to such things any more.

A Brass Razoo

(Set in the 1980s, when video recorders were state-of-the-art and you could still smoke in enclosed public spaces.)

The pub was abuzz with the din of thirsty throats washing away the day's drudgery. Pay nights were particularly good at the Hamer Club, 21st Supply Battalion. First there was the happy hour, when beer flowed cheaper, and longer, than any civilian establishment could ever match. Then came the chook raffle with its prizes of legs of ham, fattened turkeys and slabs of beer, followed later in the evening by the eagerly awaited auction. Goods ranged from digital watches, shiny military bugles and cutlery sets, to coffee machines, transistor radios and even the odd video recorder.

At our table sat Willy, an Englishman with a slow benevolent air and a propensity to talk to anyone about anything. He drank shandies with 'just a dribble of beer'.

Next to him sat Sly, a cheery bloke with a charmingly mischievous manner about him. He guzzled pints of beer with the easy grace of someone well on their way to becoming an alcoholic.

Our boss, Tommo, an adventurer with an instinctive intelligence as sharp as the knife in the leather holster on his belt, and who worked to fulfil his dream of owning a campervan in which to trek around Australia, huddled with Debbie, one of his many casual lovers. She was one of the receptionists on the base.

At the end of the table sat Slugger, a heavy drinker who smoked like a chimney, never smiled and rarely said anything. One sensed by the beer-dazed severity of the look on his face he was best left alone.

Beside him, his legs splayed and his fists pressed firmly on his knees, hunched the hulking figure of Big Ed, an ex-digger who, like many of the stores personnel who'd left the army, spent his life in civvy street working for the army. His was a taunting wit that landed him in all sorts of hot water. He'd already been slashed across his left cheek in a pub brawl because of his insolent tongue and just last week had to punch out a digger who, ruffled by his unrelenting mockery, took a swing at him. His big bald head with a dark black swath of hair around it, his thick drooping moustache and mordant eyes fixed in a suspicious squint, not to mention his impressive facial scar, were enough to warn any man with half a brain to approach him with extreme caution. It wasn't always possible to avoid him but whatever you did you never, but never, brought up the subject of baldness in his presence. He went around with a military issue beanie on his protrusive cranium.

Then there was me, straight out of year twelve, the youngest and shyest of them all. I couldn't compete with their ready sarcasm or willingness to resort to brawn at the slightest provocation and so I quietly drank as copiously as they did by way of indirect communion, though not too quietly because that would draw attention to you, throwing in the odd remark where possible. This was tolerable to most of them.

'You seen that bitch Smithy's married to, Major Stilten-Smith she calls herself?' said Big Ed to Slugger. 'Walks like she's got a dildo stuck up her arse. Stilten is right, the crusty old lump of cheese!' Pouting his lips with a grotesquely supercilious air he believed reflected her manner, he sneered, '"I think your storehouse needs to be reorganised to get your tardy despatch procedures up to scratch to meet current demands…" Jesus, she couldn't tell a forklift from a silver spoon if ya served her breakfast with one an' she's tellin' me how to run me storehouse! Fuckin' 'ell, how does Smithy put up with it? If it was up to me, I'd show 'er what that big mouth of 'ers is good for!'

Smithy was the warrant officer responsible for the storehouse adjacent to Big Ed's.

Slugger remained unmoved.

Sly interjected, 'D'yer reckon she gets him to stand to attention in bed?'

We laughed.

Emboldened, he continued, '"Your weapon's not up to scratch, Warrant Officer Smith. Needs a good spit and polish. Here, let me show you how. Spurrt! There, see how beautiful and shiny it comes up! Come on then! Now, get your aim right. No, not like that, hit the target…like this…ah…that's better, step it up, step it up, not so tardy now! I want repeated rounds right on the button!"'

Then Sly, heaving and panting in his seat, assuming an overtaxed voice struggling against exhaustion said, '"Like this, ma'am? Is this okay, ma'am?"' Panting, sighing and groaning histrionically, he answered his own question in a husky feminine voice, '"Oh yes, oh yes, Warrant Officer Smith. Now slaughter me like the fat, horny bush pig I am and stick that bayonet right in here where it hurts! Arrrhhh,"' he concluded, rolling his eyes grotesquely as if fading in a deadly swoon. '"Arrrhhh!"'

The others, with the exception of Slugger and Willy, chuckled maliciously. Slugger put his beer pot down and kept his gaze fixed on Sly for the duration of his farce, perhaps the closest token of approval one was likely to get from someone who would otherwise ignore you. Willy shook his head in disbelief.

'What's up with you, old timer?' Tommo asked Willy light-heartedly.

''Tisn't good form to knock yer workmates like that, 'specially a good bloke like Smithy. And sure, the major needs a few creases ironed out of her, but she's just a bit green around the ears… In any case, you should always treat yer superiors with respect, especially a woman.'

They shook their heads dismissively at Willy's bygone sense of chivalry.

'Hey, Scout!' shouted Sly across the room.

Scout looked over and made his way to us with a drunken waddle. He was a well-liked easy-going digger who never gave anyone any strife. Resourceful, competent at his job and bloody handy with a hammer, he could get any broken-down piece of junk going despite its missing parts. His one failing was the drink and though he kept his professional and recreational lives separate, did more than was expected and was never insubordinate, his superiors couldn't have failed to notice this. No doubt that was why at thirty-eight, after twenty years in the army, he'd never got past corporal. It didn't seem to bother him one bit.

His merry face, mottled with red alcoholic blotches, smiled at us. 'G'day, all!'

'Yer still standin',' mocked Big Ed.

Scout blinked, ran his hand reflectively over his bald flaking pate and said with a drunken sway, 'Only half whacked at the moment but the night's still young… It's really buzzin' tonight… See, I won the turkey before.' He frowned briefly. 'Would've preferred the slab but at least the missus'll be impressed,' he said with a troubled ripple of his brow.

'Here's that fifty I owe ya. Thanks, mate!' said Sly.

'No worries,' nodded Scout. 'I'd better get back to Chook and Jonesy. Check yas later.' He wove a crooked line through the congeries of bodies back to his mates.

'Don't worry! It'll probably never happen,' said Willy warmly to me.

He startled me out of my thoughts. This was a humorous expression used about the battalion when one was silent or reflective but since a few people had said it to me recently, I wondered if I went around with a troubled look on my face. I did have a tendency to crease my forehead for no apparent reason.

'He's all right,' said Tommo. 'Probably busy hatching the plot of his next blockbuster.'

Big Ed looked up curiously.

'He's a writer when he's not a storeman,' Tommo continued by way of explanation.

'Writer? What the hell does he write then?' asked Big Ed.

Oversensitive and uneasy about where the conversation might lead, I was about to interpose with 'stories', but Tommo beat me to the punch.

'Poetry. This grimy worker you see before you is nothing less than a budding poet,' he said with a smirk.

'Poetry? Yeah?' quizzed Big Ed with an unexpected and reassuring look of genuine interest on his face. 'I read the stuff all the time! You got a girlfriend, Fred?'

I shook my head.

He extended his arms out, limped his wrists and bobbed up and down on his seat. 'Nah, of course not! Too busy traipsing about smelling the fuckin' roses when you should be out sniffin' for a bitta beaver!' He put his arms down. 'Jesus, if you were my kid, I'd give ya a good clip over the ear for gettin' into that poofy stuff! Bloody po-et-ry,' he sneered, shoving his empty glass away contemptuously before getting up to fetch another drink.

'Man's gotta have a hobby,' I said as nonchalantly as I could to save face as he walked away.

I regretted that I'd ever mentioned it to Tommo. I should have known better. Nothing remained private there for long. Everyone knew everyone else's business sooner or later. Everyone knew who was sleeping with whom and cheating on whom, with the exception of the blissful fool who was being cheated on and whom everyone secretly sniggered about. I looked at Tommo's girl, Debbie, and remembered the background to this little liaison, none of which was my business but which Tommo himself gleefully insisted on divulging to me.

Debbie had been infatuated with Sly, who, finding her tiresome, wanted nothing to do with her. I'd noticed this myself. So, Tommo told me, he and Sly had agreed that he would woo her away to their mutual benefit. She would leave Sly alone and Tommo would enjoy the spoils. As far as Tommo was concerned, anything with a heartbeat was fair game for the sack and I'd seen him with some real shockers in the past, though in this case, I must say, his prize wasn't altogether bad. Debbie was in the main a good-looker.

When Tommo first told me of their little conspiracy, I thought it was all talk, mere masculine boasting intended to display his prowess in matters of seduction to impress the other guys. He definitely saw himself as a bit of a Casanova. Well, it wasn't too long before he'd achieved what he set out to do. At the pub, she hung around him like a bad smell and couldn't take her eyes, or hands, off him. I sort of felt sorry for her as I recollected Sly and Tommo's pact. To Tommo, it was all a game, a bit of fun on the side because, whatever happened, he'd always return to his regular partner and kids in the end, but she was really smitten and no doubt flattered that someone as magnetic as him had paid her court. That's the way it was there. Except for her, the victim, everyone else knew the sorry truth, and knew too the secret contempt a conspirator usually feels for someone too foolish to see they're being duped by the very hand they lap like a loyal dog.

'And now,' I thought ruefully, 'Big Ed'll mock me with his "po-et-ry" every time he sees me until it'll become a running joke all over the army camp – "Fred the pansy poet". Oh well, I'll just have to grin and bear it and act like I don't care…'

'Hey, there's that horny recruit, with special emphasis on the root! What a honey!' said Sly.

I looked up to see Private Lisa Crompton. My heart jumped! I couldn't agree more with Sly's crass assessment. Though I relished the cheap beer, she was the secret reason I bothered with the happy hours. The thought of catching a glimpse of her or even exchanging a few words thrilled me.

Lisa was a wide-eyed girl from Perth who'd been working in my storehouse the last three months. We got on well and I sensed there was some interest on her part towards me but, being the diffident fool I was, I explained that away as wishful thinking. It was a delicious mixture of pain and happiness I felt whenever I saw her. As far as I was concerned, she possessed all the attributes that made a woman beautiful. But it wasn't just a carnal attraction that I found exciting, irresistible as that was, it was also her open and sensitive character, her adventurous and yet thoughtful attitude when, in between sorting stock, we joked and talked about what was most important to us. Ill-adapted and awkward,

I, who generally felt nervous and remained silent around beautiful women, felt at ease with her because of a trust between us that was immediate. I could let myself go a bit and share things with her we cared about so that I convinced myself I knew her better than the colleagues with whom she spent most of her working days. Such trust between two people was something special, I often told myself naively by way of hopeful encouragement.

And yet, whatever I told myself, I lamented the painful reality that someone so alluring would always be beyond my reach because I lacked the courage to air my feelings. I felt a longing twinge, like a blade, carving a hollow in my heart whenever she was around.

Tommo turned round. 'Hm, nice setta tits…civvies bring out the best in 'er, the overalls disguise 'em well…'

Debbie ruffled a little and said, 'Don't forget you're taken.'

'As long as I'm not taken for granted. I may have eyes for her but all my essential parts are for you!' he said gleefully.

Debbie succumbed to his cavalier charm and twittered stupidly.

'Whatta ya mean, with "emphasis on the root"?' Willy asked as if he'd just registered what Sly had said.

Before Sly could get a word out, Debbie blurted with a nod towards Lisa, 'That angel-faced bombshell is a little slut, that's what he means. I can tell ya for a fact she was a virgin when she got here, all of nineteen six months ago, but since her first taste of cock, she hasn't bin able to stop herself. A regular root-rat she's become!' She sniggered in her hand, 'You know what I heard? One of the diggers here got the clap from 'er when they were training out bush. So the medico wants to know who she's had sex with recently so they can nip it in the bud. Well, next mornin' there are fifteen guys beatin' a path to his door for treatment!'

'All with dishonourable discharges!' quipped Sly.

They roared with laughter, including Big Ed, who'd returned with a drink, his beer gut heaving tremulously like a blob of jelly. Slugger nodded vacantly, the ghost of a smirk on his lips. Only Willy shook his head silently in dismay.

That stab in my heart sharpened in intensity with Debbie's revelation and I drooped disconsolately. If I wasn't in a black mood before, I certainly was then. My night of high hopes had not only set me up as the butt of Big Ed's sarcasm from then on, but also succeeded in shooting down my naive illusions in flames. The chance to glimpse Lisa and the possibility of some brief encounter with her had been the only consolation for working in that desolate, god-forsaken battalion. Only that had made the seven thirty starts on winter mornings, my icy hands raw with having to handle cold steel in what was basically an oversized tin shed with concrete floors infested with redbacks and even the occasional tiger snake wrapped snugly among the stock, worthwhile. Now that was gone. I'd never be able to look at Lisa in quite the same way.

As Tommo and Debbie leaned against each other whispering lasciviously, I at once reviled and secretly envied Tommo, wishing that I could be as charming and uncaring. Why was it all the women in the battalion seemed to go for men who'd only use them for their amusement? Why couldn't I be like that, live for the moment and damn the consequences? But I didn't have to ask why. I knew. The women there were attracted to a man confident in himself. They expected him to claim what he wanted assertively. That was a sign of real masculinity in their eyes. It wasn't a mystery that someone like Tommo should have so much success. First, he didn't have any taste, and second, he was full of himself and these women liked that. The last thing they wanted was a bleeding heart whose naive romanticism expected more of them than they had to offer. They wanted men of action, not dreamers, a brute and sweaty carnal coupling and not some flaccid eulogy to undying love. They felt uneasy with any such sensitivity and mistrusted it because it seemed too airy-fairy, too uncertain – too weak.

Maybe Willy sensed my ill-humour and may have even gleaned its cause because he said, 'Fred, mate, things are never as bad as they seem. Let me tell you a story about someone I knew a long time back. Now you may say this is all a load of old cobblers but I assure you, it's as true as the light of day.

'Now, this bloke migrated from Britain nigh on thirty-two year ago, when he was just in his twenties, because he'd heard Australia was a land of opportunity. Besides, he found the foul English weather, for all of its wild beauty, mostly depressing. He wanted sun, lots of it, and space for his youthful ambitions, and most of all, a fresh start! In short, like most blokes his age, he was a romantic fool.

'So there he was in a strange land with no friends or relatives to support him, just himself, his wife and their little 'un. Now, virtually from day one, this bloke regretted his move. He hated Australia! He found the place harsh and Australians generally narrow-minded. He couldn't help feeling they had a pretty big chip on their shoulder because he just had to open his mouth to get short shrift. It didn't matter so much what he said, how sensible it was, as the way he spoke, the fact he sounded different, that's all that seemed to matter to 'em. Day in day out, they couldn't resist knockin' 'im by remindin' 'im of his foreignness. "Bloody pom this, bloody pom that," that's all he remembers hearing from 'em. You see, they didn't see him as just another bloke strugglin' to make his way through the rough and tumble of the world but as something strange, comical even, almost somethin' to be feared and mocked. And there was always a certain mightier-than-thou attitude in the way they addressed him, as if he were a fool just by virtue of his nationality. He only realised later that maybe this was just a way of covering up their own insecurity, their fear of the unknown. Australia in the fifties was still pretty provincial, if ya know what I mean, and it's easier to laugh somethin' off that's challengin' than make the hard effort to understand it. He was a simple man, so he couldn't say for sure but that was his gut feeling.

'But he noticed too, the Italians, Greeks and other nationalities got similar treatment. I tell a lie. In fact, they was worse off because most of the poor beggars couldn't even speak English. Actually, he was better tolerated. But he felt more akin to them, the "wogs" they called 'em, than he did to most Aussies, even if he couldn't understand a bloody word they was sayin' to 'im most of the time.

'So this Englishman felt pretty alone and the first year of his life in the promised land was dismal, sheer hell. His wife felt the same and nagged him about gettin' back home. He didn't want to give up so soon but in any case couldn't return even if he wanted to until he'd saved enough money for their return passages.

'Well, the strangeness of the new land and its ways, the drudgery of working two factory jobs, his sense of entrapment, the wife's constant discontent and savage nagging, it all took its toll and he started seeking solace in the last place to find it – the bottle. Well, as you can imagine, that only made his wife unhappier than ever and fiercer in her hostility towards him. He struggled to keep her happy but in the end turned a deaf and defeated ear to her and pretty much sleepwalked through his days.

'He'd already lost one job for turning up late several times with alcohol on his breath. Eventually, he lost the other one too from sheer exhaustion. You see, they caught him sleeping on the job and no wonder too with that monotonous drone of the conveyor belt and constant click-clack, click-clack of the canning machine he was supposed to oversee poundin' in his head.

'After that, things really hotted up between him and his wife. She blamed him for all her troubles and he secretly agreed. One day, he got back home to find her gone. He wasn't altogether surprised. For years after, he never knew where she'd skedaddled off to until he got word she'd shacked up with someone who could give her everything she wanted. She'd made it back to England with her lover and was happy with her lot. She'd found her luck, he thought, and was glad for her. It was better that way. He was obviously unlucky and there was no tellin' when the black cloud that seemed to follow him everywhere would finally lift.

'He thought to himself, "Hell, I've lost me loved ones and me jobs! These things usually happen in threes. I wonder what's in store around the corner?" Well, where his judgement about Australia being a land of milk and honey had proved, to say the least, optimistic, as did his dream of the luxurious future he and his wife would share in the promised land, he was right on the money about that third piece of bad luck coming his way.

'Within a week of his wife's desertion, his health began failing. He started feeling a kind of tightness in his temple and when he tried to read the papers, the print got fuzzy. Suddenly, he had blindin' headaches that left him feelin' poorly. Along with them, a debilitating weariness left him flat on his back on the couch. One day, he was walking down the street when a strange feeling overcame him. He felt weak. His legs began shaking uncontrollably and he had to lean against a rail for support. Like in a bad dream, he tried to scream for help but couldn't even muster the strength to manage that. Before he knew it, he collapsed.

'He woke up in hospital to find he'd had an aneurism in the brain. He was extremely fortunate they got to him in time, the doctor told him. Just a tad longer without treatment and it would have been much worse.

'"Lucky, damned lucky!" his doctor repeated with a nod.

'"Well, there's a first time for everything!" he thought wryly to himself.

'After two weeks in hospital, he was discharged with strict orders not to exert himself for the next year and to keep off the tobacco and booze. He'd suffered some impairment to his coordination but with six months of rehab, he pretty much got back up to scratch. In any case, there was nothing for it, he had to swallow his pride and do what he promised himself he never would – join the dole queue. This final humiliation, he felt, was the lowest ebb in his life.

'As he walked the streets aimlessly, lost in his dark thoughts, he recounted his time in Australia, how his feeling of being rootless had remained unchanged, in fact worsened. How he'd lost his wife and son forever, lost his jobs and now even his health, which was by no means assured despite the successful outcome of his treatment, all the while lamenting that he didn't even have enough money for one measly passage back to little ol' England. He'd just crossed Princess Bridge when the thought of throwing himself into the Yarra crossed his mind. All he had to do was direct his body to the concrete base of the pylon, just make sure he smashed his skull against it. It would be so simple, so easy, one moment of fear and then eternal peace.

'"Simple? Knowing me luck, I'd even bungle that and probably end up a quadriplegic or somethin'," he thought bitterly.

'"And keep off the smokes and booze!" His doctor's admonition flashed through his mind, its authoritative tone tinged with the defeated annoyance of his own self-mocking voice. He turned his pocket inside-out and surveying the lint and tobacco dregs on the lining, thought, "With a pocketful of nothin', I'll certainly manage that at least."

'He wasn't the type to wallow in self-pity but at that moment felt like falling to his knees and breaking down into a raging and uncontrollable sob. And maybe at just that moment, unbeknownst to him, something like an involuntary prayer slipped out as a plea for help despite himself. He stuffed the lining of his pocket back into his trousers with a self-loathing he'd never thought himself capable of and muttered angrily, "I don't even have a bloody brass razoo to me name!"

'Just then, he saw something glinting in the gutter. He walked up to it, stooped over and picked it up. It looked like an old Australian penny. He wiped the grime off with his thumb and made out the effigy of a kangaroo. Then he stopped aghast as he whispered the inscription around its border to himself in disbelief. It read, "Not even worth a brass razoo". Turning it over, the same mock effigy of an Australian penny and inscription adorned its other side. He stood there dumbstruck looking at the scratched and beaten piece of metal with bewildered excitement. The hair on the back of his neck stood up as he stared at it. That he should find this fake coin, this comical artefact, at the very moment he'd thought what he had, seemed so remote from the bounds of probability that it was almost like a miracle. A smile escaped his lips. For the first time in a year, he remembered what it was like to feel human, a moment of levity like, 'cause this was surely a good sign and promised something no man can live without – hope. A feeling of lightness, joy even, rippled through him and he knew that he had hit rock bottom and from then on things could only get better…'

'Then he crossed the road and got run over by a semi!' Big Ed interjected drolly with impeccable timing.

We laughed.

'No,' continued Willy sternly. 'No,' his voice softened. 'Things panned out just the way he thought they would. He cleaned himself up, got a job and stayed on in Australia. He even got to like Australians, brazen rabble that they are, and wouldn't live anywhere else in the world,' he said, smiling affectionately to Big Ed. 'You see,' he continued thoughtfully, 'his problem was he was tryin' too hard, thinkin' it was all up to him, but he realised that day that you can only do what the powers that be allow you. Call it fate or fortune, who knows, none of us is master of his destiny. It's by a higher grace we're granted our time with all its trials and tribulations and, however dark things seem, an open door is there for all of us, so long as we're not so big-headed as to refuse it. Nah, when he thought he had nothin', he finds this token, in itself worth nothin', that, ironic like, affirms and yet contradicts everythin' he's mopin' about. It was like a consoling tap on the shoulder from some invisible hand that seemed to say, "Well, now at least you have a tangible nothin'!" He couldn't but help feel reassured that if something like a higher power, a God say, exists, He certainly had a sense of humour and had shared His little joke with him,' he concluded with a nod and generous wink to me.

'Sounds like a load of old cobblers, if ya ask me.' Big Ed mimicked Willy's familiar expression.

'Yeah, I think your English friend was having you on, Willy,' agreed Tommo.

'Oh yeah?' Willy intoned knowingly. He shifted his weight to one side of his rump and from the back trouser pocket of the other pulled out his wallet. He opened it, unclipped one compartment and withdrew what looked like an old copper penny. 'That's the very thing! I've kept it with me ever since.'

We passed it around till it came to me. It was, as he had recounted, a scratched and beaten coin with the said inscription. I ran my thumb over the scratches and thought of the deep creases that lined old Willy's tired face. I sat there at once entranced by the improbability of Willy's account and my conviction in its absolute veracity. And yet, impressive as his story was, when I compared the earnestness of Willy's voice, the sense of purpose it reflected, with the outcome of that turning point in his life which had led, ultimately, to our shabby table and a life of futile drudgery shared with a lot of hard men and women who did nothing more than get drunk and fornicate at every opportunity, I couldn't suppress a feeling of desolation. Even now, I sensed they thought him a fool for his sincere disclosure and I felt queasy by the mixture of alcohol and obdurate cynicism of the moment. I handed the copper back to Willy and he took it with a triumphant glint in his eye.

The room was beginning to spin when I closed my tired eyes. Opening them only made it lurch fuzzily in the bright light. I breathed deeply and quietly so as not to be obvious for temporary relief.

'Seven thirty! Must be gettin' close to Flo's entrance time,' said Sly with a smirk.

They turned around in the direction of the bar. To the left of it, on his rump, his back against the wall and his legs splayed, Scout sat unconscious with one arm wrapped around his frozen turkey. He snored as his head drooped forward and spittle dribbled down his chin and onto his khaki shirt.

'Give 'er another five minutes, I reckon,' said Tommo.

'Dead-set weak as piss, old Scout is. Didn't even last the distance to the auction,' jeered Big Ed.

Just then, a large blonde woman entered the pub and paced deliberately up to Scout.

'There she is, right on the dot,' said Sly.

She squatted beside Scout, shifted his weight onto one buttock, not without tenderness, and removed his wallet. She pulled out the notes, counted them and put one hundred back in. She replaced his wallet in his back pocket while Scout made bewildered gurgling noises. She straightened and steadied him against the wall, stood up with one swift motion, turned and, without acknowledging anyone, exited.

I watched him lying there like a helpless infant with his arm wrapped around his turkey as if it were a teddy bear. It was almost as if his mummy had walked in, taken away some dangerous object not suitable for him to play with, put a soft toy in for reassurance and tucked him soundly in his cot. We all knew Flo had to do this because Scout's thirst would eventually rouse him again and, left to his own devices, he would blow a substantial sum of his pay on drink. She had done what was necessary in her perfunctory way to spare him and herself any humiliation, which was why her gaze avoided crossing anyone else's. Still, a wave of embarrassment and empathy stirred in me for him. It wasn't just that he looked ridiculous as his spluttering lips made raspberries with each exhalation, it was also because the idea that a woman 'wore the pants' was reason enough to provoke the bitter scorn of men like Slugger and Big Ed even though they themselves, being the overgrown boys they were, were probably just as answerable to their wives behind closed doors. Then again, maybe not. I could imagine someone like Slugger just clobbering his protesting wife in a drunken rage.

Sadie walked up to our table and stood beside Sly. She was a woman in her mid-forties who'd worked for the army in various civilian roles for fifteen years. The life suited her rough blokey temperament. She had a wrinkled face over-made with rouge and pale foundation so that it looked like it belonged to a ragged kewpie doll. Buxom, she wore a checked flannel shirt tucked into faded jeans that seemed at least two sizes too small for her. Her figure was still quite good for her age, though the incipient bulges showing through the denim at her hips suggested inevitable decline. With one hand on a stubby and the other holding a cigarette, she struck up a conversation with Sly.

Earlier in the evening, I'd offered to buy her a drink out of politeness as we worked together in Storehouse Four.

She had replied that someone on my wage couldn't afford her particular preferences. 'I drink Campari or gin and tonic,' she'd said as if these signified some universally recognised mark of rare sophistication.

Having committed myself, I insisted anyway. Evidently, knockin' those drinks back at the rate she did had become too expensive even for someone on her wage or, maybe, she'd had her fill of the harder stuff and was goin' for something lighter… She stood there in her steel-capped boots, the weight of her body falling on one hip so that its complementary hip protruded, accentuating its feminine curve.

'Yer still here! Isn't it past yer bedtime?' she quipped to me.

'I don't know. You got the time?' I replied awkwardly.

'Yeah, you got the inclination?' she said, with her eyes fixed in a lascivious squint on me.

At a loss for a glib response, I smiled back innocuously. She pouted her lips and sucked greedily on her stubby.

'Yer barkin' up the wrong tree there, Sadie. That there is a poet!' said Big Ed morosely, limping his wrist and running his hand over his brow with tortured hyperbole.

She withdrew the stubby from her lips and cackled loudly, accompanied by one or two other chuckles from the table. As she shuddered with laughter, her excessive bust heaving conspicuously, I reflected on that leer she'd just given me. She was always making lewd, suggestive comments to me and I often wondered if there was anything more in them than just her crude sense of humour. Incorrigibly flirtatious, especially with the younger men, even now her convulsing body had moved in closer to where Sly was seated and rubbed against him. At twenty-seven, he was the next youngest at our table after me and there was no denying he cut a handsome figure. She eventually stopped and, stooping over, continued talking with him.

Just before the auction began, we scrambled for refills. My mood still hadn't improved and I felt bored. It only got worse when my gaze happened to fall on Lisa to see her flirting with one of the diggers. A paragon of masculinity with broad shoulders, even chiselled features and a quiet self-assurance, one could hardly blame her. In a moment of distraction, I responded to something Willy had said with a gesture of my hand. The auctioneer took it for a bid and I found myself the owner of an ugly digital watch. The telling silence in the room as the auctioneer struggled to offload that piece of junk, and the ten dollars more than it was worth I'd inadvertently bid, no doubt in most people's eyes left me looking like a fool who didn't understand the value of his hard-earned cash. After my mistake, I waited in agony for someone to outbid me but I might as well have waited for a friendly word from Big Ed. So the auction proceeded with, generally, useless item after useless item flogged off for a pittance. To avoid a similar mistake, I folded my arms and sat dejectedly in silence. At the end of the auction, I reluctantly forked out thirty-five dollars and collected my prize.

I was having one for the road when Davo came up to me with his arm in a sling. Like a lot of the diggers who'd ended up in Ordnance, he'd had visions of an exciting career in the infantry, only to discover he was colour-blind, or had a crook back or bung knee or whatever else made him unsuitable for a combat role. In his case, he had several elusive ailments that seemed to manifest periodically, especially when hard work was demanded. This in no way compromised his vision of himself as a model of marshal masculinity.

'Hi, Fred. Got yerself a nice watch there. I went for it myself but you outbid me.'

'What's wrong with the arm?'

'Sprained it wresting with Todd during exercises…got me by surprise, still that's part and parcel of the work we do,' he said self-importantly, drawing on his durry. 'Can I 'ave a look at it, see what I missed out on?'

I passed the watch to him and he gloated over it. 'Gee, it's beautiful! I'm sick of this wind-up one of mine, keeps losing time.'

In his loud Hawaiian shirt, his cheap jeans and tasteless runners, I wasn't at all surprised he saw a certain beauty in that piece of rubbish.

'It's yours!' I said.

'Mine? Ah nah, Fred, I couldn't!'

'I don't know why I bought it. I don't even like digital watches. Take it and enjoy it.'

'Aw, gee, thanks, mate. Ya sure? Gee, thanks… I'll have to buy ya a jar…'

Looking around at Scout, now babbling incoherently and waving his hand wildly as if he conducted an imaginary band, occasionally raising a stern finger and paternally admonishing his frozen turkey, and Big Ed, shaking his head and telling Slugger about some 'weirdo' on the base who'd discovered he was really a woman and was going to have the dreaded 'snip', but who still had to get final approval for his operation from his psychiatrist after having lived the life of a woman for a year first, dressing and interacting as one and so on, and Tommo and Debbie luridly fondling and French-kissing each other, and Lisa, drunkenly staggering out with her lay for the night, and Davo in raptures over a useless watch that would break down in three months, if that, and, in the midst of it all, Willy, smiling benignly to himself like a good-natured simpleton, his life redeemed by a fake copper coin carried on his person like a crucifix, I felt an oppressive and desolate sense of loneliness mingled with absurdity.

'Nah, thanks, Davo,' I said standing up. 'I've gotta go. Get me a drink some other time. Goodbye, all!'

I noticed that Sly and Sadie had disappeared and, looking around, added, 'Say goodbye to Sly for me.'

'Yer not goin' already, are yer, Fred?' asked Willy.

I nodded.

Big Ed interrupted his monologue with Slugger to say, 'Of course, he's got to go home to write his po-et-try!'

'Aw, leave the kid alone, Ed. And a worthy thing it is too. Good on ya, Fred!' Willy winked at me. Then as I turned to go he added as an afterthought, 'Hey, Fred, maybe one day you can write down me story about the brass razoo! It'd make a cracker!'

There I was full of youthful ambition out of all proportion to my abilities, my head stuffed with Dostoyevsky and Maupassant and Kafka, and humble old Willy entertaining the thought that I would see anything more significant in his tale than a quirky piece of barroom babble. I nodded with just enough feigned enthusiasm to suggest the possibility that I took him seriously.

Outside the smoke-filled room, the air was clear and fresh. My eyes burned. It was a beautiful night and the stars shone distinctly. Setting off, the undulating babble of the revellers and the warm glow of the windows grew more alluring as they receded into darkened silence. I rounded the corner on my way towards the gates when I heard something stir. I squinted and looked towards a recess in the wall. There, faintly outlined in the glow falling obliquely from an overhead light, I saw a figure bundled in the shadows. As my eyes adjusted, I saw Sadie on her knees, her head sliding backwards and forwards with a steady motion. Out of the darkness came intermittent moans. Barely visible, leaning against the wall in the shadows over her, stood the figure of a tall man. It looked like Sly. I moved away discreetly.

The walk back home was as always long and lonely. The pock-marked streets and shabby housing commission estates, leaning into the night, looked tired and sad in the dirty glow of the neon. They looked worse in daylight. As cars hissed by from behind me or turned into side streets at my rear, I stared at the squiggly shadows of the trees cast from their headlights spreading out like trails of crooked ink streaming in a vertiginous web across the footpath and lawns. To my drunken fancy, they appeared like the pulsing tentacles of some dark sea creature emerging from its lair and reaching for something in the inconsolable night. I tried to capture the vague feel of it all and fell to turning doggerel in my addled mind.

My throat dry and feeling hungry, I approached a Seven Eleven store. I pulled out my wallet and flicked through the notes only to re-alise I'd blown nearly half my pay. Dismayed, I thrust it back in my pocket and kept walking, dissatisfied with the way the night had turned out and saddened by the bleak prospects my first real job foreshadowed.

'How can they live like that,' I thought, 'slogging it out day after futile day to a fabled retirement when, bored with themselves and finally confronted by the vacuity of their lives, they drop off their perches into oblivion from sheer tedium – without poetry, without fascination for the wonder of it all? Without a simple acceptance that life isn't pulling a fast one on 'em and that a man doesn't have to pretend he's got it all in hand no matter what, and hey, that even a little naiveté's not such a bad thing? At least Willy's got that. Maybe it comes with age? Maybe one has to find that door that's waiting for us Willy was on about? To hell with them if they thought him a fool! To hell with me too!'

I turned into an alley, the cobblestones lit only by the muted moonlight. Fallen leaves and tiny shards of glass glittered and sparkled before me. Annoyed and angry at myself, lonely and lustful, I thought about Willy and wondered if perhaps there might not be a brass razoo lying somewhere waiting for me to pick up.

The Visitation

He had been feeling rundown lately, probably because he hadn't been sleeping so well. On his way to the office, the idea of having to sit there all day at his desk checking statistics and writing reports made his eyes heavy with fatigue. Normally, there would be no question of his getting through a day efficiently but for the past few weeks he could muster little enthusiasm for it. True, his job had always been a means to an end, never a passion, but he did it professionally and did it well and there was usually some satisfaction in that. No, something was wrong because he even lacked the desire for what was indeed a passion, reading great literature when he got home or viewing paintings at every opportunity or investigating what was happening around town in the wide and wonderful world of local arts.

Putting down his bag and doffing his coat, he sat at his desk, surveyed it attentively, and knew things had been, once again, tampered with. He looked for the pen he'd left in its usual spot yesterday afternoon but couldn't find it. He sighed and stared ahead, not quite knowing what to do – he never did. He was, after all, a retiring man who really didn't expect – nor certainly demand – much from life apart from that it would behave itself and allow him to go along a relatively unimpeded trajectory. That's what people implicitly expect and he, like the meekest of them, felt anxious when that perfectly normal expectation proved unwarranted.

'Is something wrong, Laurie?' a voice addressed him.

He turned to see Barry smiling disingenuously at him. He knew it was Barry who had rearranged his desk just for the nuisance of it and who, for some reason, had always had it in for him. From their first meeting when Laurie had stepped up to him and extended his hand in a spirit of welcoming colleagueship, Barry had taken a disliking to him. Why, he didn't know, nor why he seemed to relish making life as difficult as possible for someone who had actually done him no wrong nor bore him any malice.

Barry was a handsome, athletically built man in his thirties, at least fifteen years younger than Laurie, who considered just about everybody his inferior. His was a swaggering push-and-shove approach bound to demoralise gentler sensibilities like Laurie's, particularly since his cavalier attitude of riding roughshod over any quaint notions of modesty fell by the wayside while he went along in his inconsiderate and successful way without consequence. Many of the women they worked with found his self-assurance charming and he relished nothing better than exercising his narcissism by wheedling himself into their confidence, especially the more cautious amongst them who had been initially reserved towards him.

He loved playing pranks on people just to see how far he could push them and the more susceptible he sensed someone's vulnerability, the more relentlessly was he likely to up the ante for the amusement of it. In the case of Laurie, though, there was something more than mere mischief involved, something really quite unpalatable; it was as if Laurie's very inoffensiveness, his deference and politeness to others taken even to the point of self-effacement, roused Barry's contempt so that he considered him some sort of insignificant thing and, as such, a worthy target on which he could easily augment his already inflated sense of superiority.

Like a cornered prey about to be pounced, Laurie didn't know how to respond as he struggled to endure the sarcastically provocative look of feigned concern Barry trained on him, as if in expectation of a reply, and which Barry knew would add an ingredient of tension, even torture, to his visible unease. Looking away meekly, Laurie felt a helpless rage as Barry openly, if not conspicuously, insulted him by just that look.

Then, just to exacerbate Laurie's sense of entrapment, Barry turned to his colleague, Gary, a flunkey of sorts and born follower, and said, 'The poor guy's a bit off colour, looks like he's seen a ghost or something.'

'More like a poltergeist, I reckon. They've got a reputation for shifting things about,' Gary sniggered to Barry in sycophantic laudation of his puerile pranks. 'Look, it seems he's even lost his tongue…'

Laurie's anger quite inexplicably dissipated and an emotion more akin to fear overtook him with the mere mentioning of ghosts. He was not a superstitious man but something like a deep-seated dread sat heavily in his stomach with the enunciation of that word. The need to distract himself from that fearful evocation, that most especially, along with his inability to redress an anger that entailed an assertiveness of which he felt incapable, compelled him to wave his hand dismissively at the futility of it all, get up and make his way to the bathroom where he could remain quarantined from the vulgarity of his colleagues.

Barry and Gary, amused by the result of their mockery, smirked at each other with malicious satisfaction.

At home that evening in the quiet solitude of his study, Laurie had intended to stay up reading but, as had been happening recently, drifted off to sleep, only to be jolted awake with the sensation of falling as his head drooped forward. He started awake on one occasion and thought he'd heard a thud. Groggily rubbing his eyes, he looked at the clock to see it was a quarter to twelve and sat listening, wondering if he'd actually heard anything. He thought he was perhaps still in a state of drowsiness on its transition to full wakefulness and explained that sound away. But then there was a clearly audible shuffle to his left compelling him to look in that direction, a sound which revealed nothing peculiar yet made the hairs on the back of his neck stand on end. Ridiculous as it was, he wondered if there was an invisible presence of some kind observing him. He was tired, very tired, he told himself, then switched off the light and went to bed.

This occasional feeling of being scrutinised continued to trouble

Laurie over the following weeks. But it wasn't only that. He would hear sounds at night he couldn't explain and, from time to time, things would disappear and then turn up again somewhere other than where he remembered placing them. He wondered if he were just becoming forgetful. The other thing amid all these uncanny happenings that bothered him most was his inability to get a solid night's sleep and he mused if all the seemingly strange phenomena he had been experiencing were merely the consequence of his growing exhaustion. To sleep – oh, how he just wanted to sleep!

Whenever he managed to approach anything like a deep sleep, there was inevitably something that disturbed it. He would feel as though some presence depressed the bed with its weight or even lay on top of him. Though apparently conscious, he would lay there terrified, drenched in sweat, feeling smothered and breathless, without the ability to scream as he struggled with all his might to do so. When he awoke in the morning, he would find the bedding twisted around him like a straightjacket or hanging over the bed in disarray.

This situation was taking its toll because one day at work, cranky with weariness, Laurie was provoked into acting uncharacteristically. Again, Barry had played his annoying pranks and when, with unctuous solicitude, he taunted Laurie by asking him if everything was okay, Laurie flew into a rage, stood up at his desk and shrieked at the top of his voice, 'Stop haunting me or so help me, I'll…!'

He stopped short of concluding his sentence, conscious of the hush that had descended over the office and the shocked looks of his colleagues trained on him while he stood there awkwardly, embarrassed by his outburst. Just then, he noticed his manager looking at him with an interrogative squint and, trembling with a mixture of outrage and fear, sank back in his seat submissively. Barry raised an eyebrow with surprised amusement at the unexpected outburst he'd engendered but remained unruffled and, smiling smugly, turned to his paperwork as if nothing of the least significance had happened.

After that, there were whispers about Laurie circulating around the office. Such things as, wasn't he a strange man, this loner, who never gave anything of himself away and was so hard to get to know; who never engaged with anyone like a normal person, nor turned up to any of the social functions and who, by some tenuous implication, had a deep, disturbing secret he was hiding from everyone, unlike themselves who were, of course, perfectly open books and had nothing so human as a deep, disturbing or simply sordid secret to hide, and so on…

Barry milked it for all it was worth, using it as a means to attract the better-looking women who were busybodies with superlative manipulation. Oh, how he'd been victimised by that strange man, he'd insinuate vulnerably and yes, as he no doubt knew would happen, how willing many of those well-meaning women were to console this handsome, sensitive man who'd been so callously wronged.

That wasn't enough for Barry, though. He filed a complaint against Laurie, claiming he felt physically threatened by him. What people had witnessed, he said, was the culmination of months of subtle and persistent harassment usually expressed privately so that it hadn't till that moment become conspicuous. He got Gary to corroborate this accusation and they colluded to fabricate a scenario of Laurie's purported bullying. As Laurie was essentially an unknown quantity who had no colleagues he was on close terms with and who, further, had made a disturbing spectacle of himself, his situation was precarious. In the eyes of those involved in the investigation or those who unofficially got wind of it via Barry's machinations behind the scenes, it was implicitly assumed he was the offender. It didn't matter that he had never shown himself to be hostile to anyone nor that he had an unblemished record of twenty-five years in the public service.

One night, as Laurie dozed at his desk with a head full of worries over his professional plight, he was roused from his torpor by a loud knock. He looked about in bewilderment, suddenly quite alert, and instinctively prepared to answer the front door. It was then that a book behind him fell off the bookshelf to the floor with a thud. He looked at it, shocked and fearful, wondering whether he should pick it up. He started to hear incomprehensible sounds crescendo and then diminish into silence interspersed with what seemed a distant, feminine voice whose intermittent vocalisations he couldn't sufficiently discern.

Looking at the space before him from which the sounds emanated, it appeared to ruffle as if it were a palpable fabric, like drapes agitated by something behind them producing the briefest chink before they closed again into a quivering impenetrability, or, more so perhaps, as if it were a wrinkling body of water disturbed by some as yet unseen entity of considerable force ascending from its depths to the surface.

It was then that that space, broiling turbulently before him, parted and like two divergent torrents gushed forward and flowed back continuously into the invisible source that was producing the disturbance. From the vague opening of this fluid-like parting, a space beyond space, some indefinite activity appeared to be taking place. Volatile, incipient images struggling to manifest whirled indistinctly, accompanied by what seemed a barely human wailing. He sat there transfixed in terror as vague, shifting forms apparently laboured to assemble into something tangible only to dissipate. Paralysed by a fascination draining him of volition, he began seeing the outlines of a face, torso and limbs striving to constitute themselves into some kind of unified body before dispersing and collapsing back into the void from which they sprang.

To his surprise, he could make out a woman's refracted face and the suggestion of a neck and bare shoulder discontinuing into invisibility amid the strange fluid-like substance in which she appeared partly emergent and immersed, very much like an archaeological artefact with disparate facets exposed while the bulk of it still lay encrusted in the mire of millennia.

While he could clearly see these 'facets' as they presented themselves to him, there was still something insubstantial to them. The face that had by then become discernible within the agitated fluid and momentarily fixed as an entity still struck him as having, for want of a better word, something of the quality of an image floating in space. When the front-on face of this apparition shifted into profile, there was a point at which it seemed to rapidly diminish into nothing more than a barely suggested trace like the edge of a rotated two-dimensional plane before it regained its three-dimensional clarity in the continuance of its revolution.

This was all very baffling to Laurie and he repeatedly rubbed his eyes to dispel what had to be a hallucination brought on by fatigue. His bafflement increased, however, when the figure before him, now relatively stable, if distorted, began to push its way forward through its enveloping medium towards him. He couldn't but reel back astounded when in one inexplicable moment – marvellous or grotesque he couldn't say for his perplexity – the hand of this creature broke through the fluidic membrane that enclosed it and penetrated into the space he inhabited as he sat agog at his desk, where it remained suspended and writhing with all the tangibility of a mortal hand.

He had seen quite enough and got up with a shriek to flee the room when he heard for the first time coherent speech emanating from the rupture in space.

In a hoarse whisper, a feminine voice pleaded, 'Please…help me… help me.'

This was said as the hand exerted itself to extend further into Laurie's study against the resistance of the fluidic medium.

He froze in a quandary over what to do. His instinct was to run but being a gentle man who couldn't even stomach seeing an insect struggling without the impulse to help, he stood there unable to tear his sympathetic eyes away from the prodigy before them.

Though the enveloped form he witnessed was somewhat obscured by its medium, he could in the main make it out; he could also see that it shifted about distressfully as it laboured to extricate itself from it. Raising its submerged hand so that its knuckle pressed against that of its exposed one, which it had drawn back, it attempted to clasp the membranous sac that imprisoned it and, using its counterpoising knuckles for leverage, part it. It was able to do so to the extent that Laurie glimpsed a clearly delineated naked upper torso beneath the sheath.

Through the opening, he heard another taxed and plaintive cry for help before it managed to extend its flailing hand with enough force, in spite of the elastically retracting medium, so that its shoulder and a scant portion of its panting chest lay exposed.

Laurie could hesitate no longer. He took the dressing gown draped over a chair and approached the entity. He slipped the sleeve over the exposed arm and, running his arm effortlessly through the fluidic medium and around the figure – which he felt to be as palpable as flesh – wrapped the gown modestly around its naked body as he carefully drew it out towards himself, aiding it as best he could to release itself from its fluidic cocoon.

All Laurie was aware of as he did this was the emergence of a face, a stunningly beautiful woman's face, from what appeared to be an insubstantial yet observable fluid receding over it until it glistened magnificently before him. Shining with a milky whiteness, a brilliant pallor almost translucent in its purity, Laurie gasped at the splendour of this face with its high cheekbones, wet raven hair and sable eyes wide with a mysterious trance-like stare bordered by long black lashes still beaded with moisture. Overwhelmed before those unusually large eyes and unable to free his spellbound gaze from their fascination, he grew faint. He stumbled over to his desk and leaned there, feeling as if he were about to be plunged into a deep and irresistible darkness…

Next morning, he found himself slumped over his desk. A blurry grey object obstructed his vision before he realised it was the base of his lamp lodged against his nose with the light still blaring in his face. Slowly, as his eyes sidled inquisitively in their restricted ambit, the base of the empty glass, books and strewn papers fell back into worldly definition at which he realised he must have fallen asleep at his desk. He raised his head and leaned back yawning uneasily, trying to remember why he should feel troubled. Well, he was late for work, that was one thing, but that wasn't it. Then he remembered the strange experience with the woman of the previous night. In the cold light of day, everything normal as usual, he surmised it must have been a dream. He sighed and smiled with relief when he recollected the misplaced terror he had felt.

Rubbing his bleary eyes, he heard what sounded like a low moan. He looked up quizzically and heard it again, somewhat louder and more clearly defined as one of discomfort or maybe even pain, and then yet another. He got up, stooped over his desk in the direction of their whereabouts and saw the woman of the night before in his dressing gown curled unconsciously on the floor. Immobile in his astonishment, he remained there leaning over his desk with his mouth agape.

His mind raced chaotically in search of a rational explanation for the incomprehensibility of what he witnessed, telling itself that what was before it could not possibly be real while his senses continued to contradict that judgement. Whatever the reality, he stood there mystified, rigid with apprehension and not knowing what to do.

She appeared to be breathing with difficulty, gasping restrictively, with each inhalation followed by a disturbing gurgling sound as she exhaled, as if her throat were obstructed or her chest congested. She moaned again, shuddered slightly and, coughing feebly, discharged a stream of fluid. He reeled back fearfully but quickly composed himself when he realised her need of assistance overrode all other considerations. He approached her and felt for any obstruction in her mouth, upon which another copious gush of fluid escaped. She began coughing and when that had passed, her breathing settled into normality. He kept her leaning forward on the floor to aid any further evacuation of fluid and wondered as he slapped her hands and gently tapped her face to rouse her if he should call an ambulance. But how would he begin to explain how she had come to be in this condition or even who she was? How would he account for this unknown presence or the bizarre manner of her emergence which, in any case, he could not coherently recount to himself? Thankfully, it appeared as if she were coming to. She had already partially opened her eyes once or twice and a rosy blush was returning to the livid hue of her lips.

He sat her up in his arms, shook her gently and asked her if she could hear him. This he did for some time until her eyes flickered open and those immense irises, exquisitely mysterious, stared back at him impassively from their at once strangely lustrous and ebony depths.

Laurie was not a strong man. He braced himself in expectation of the effort to pick her up and place her on his reading settee but was surprised to find there was an uncanny lightness to her frame. After doing so, he rubbed one of her hands and again asked if she could hear him. She was still succumbing to sporadic swoons, weaving in and out of wakefulness, but eventually came to fix her open eyes on him. In sudden recognition of her unfamiliar surroundings, they assumed a widened, disoriented aspect. She started and attempted to get up in a fumbling panic but Laurie pressed her back gently.

'It's okay, nothing to worry about. Can you hear me?'

She clasped the armrest with both hands and retreated rigidly back into the settee at the sound of his voice, her eyes trained fearfully on him.

'Don't be frightened. Who' – he felt like asking 'what' – 'are you?' Still receiving no response, he remained crouched beside her as his thoughts busied themselves in a tangle of uncertainty over what to do. 'Do you have a name? Can you speak? You spoke last night… didn't you?'

Amid the unbroken silence, he bowed his head with a sense of helplessness as he considered what vague options were open to him. Feeling powerless as he did so, his unsettled stomach tightened with increasing anxiety and he sighed disconsolately.

'Do you have a name?' he heard repeated in a low melodious voice.

He looked up expectantly and saw her eyes wandering searchingly as she said again to herself curiously, 'Do you have a name?'

A feeling of relief swept over him. 'You can speak!' He pointed to himself and said, 'Laurie, I'm Laurie!' Then he gestured to her, 'You, your name?'

'You can speak,' she mimicked hesitantly to herself, as if testing her ability to speak.

In his excitement, Laurie's animation frightened her and she flinched apprehensively in her still retracted posture.

He composed himself as best he could and stroked her shoulder soothingly, coaxing her to relax, and said, 'I'm sorry. Have no fear, no harm will come to you…' He stood up carefully and, retreating slowly so as not to startle her with any sudden movement, put up his hands and said, 'Stay there, I'll be back…'

The first thing he did was to call in to work to say he wouldn't be in. He was still unclear what to do next – should he seek help from someone, anyone? God knows, he wished he could. In any event, before he decided on anything, he would need some time to get acquainted with his unexpected visitor.

The next thing he thought of was getting in touch with his sister. He would have preferred to avoid her because she had a tendency to poke her nose in where it wasn't wanted, always insisting on what he should do for his own good and what she thought best for him. In this case, though, he needed to get some women's clothes and his sister's frame was not dissimilar to his guest's. Perhaps too he would need a woman's help, for he was uncertain how to tackle the problem of fitting her out with a wardrobe or attending to her toiletry. The brief encounter he had had with her so far suggested, disconcertingly so, she may be untrained in these matters. But then again the troubling question arose – how was he to explain this woman's presence? His sister would think him mad if he told her the truth. He would play it by ear and deal with that problem when it arose. Quietly fretting nonetheless, his sister's familiar phrase, 'Blood is thicker than water', came to mind, an expression she used whenever she felt compelled to impose herself in situations where she thought he was embarrassing himself or in need of someone as savvy as herself to take charge and sort things out for him.

After having called her, he took some water to his guest and sat with her. She drank it avidly and extended her glass to him for more. While still reticent, even tense, he felt she was slowly becoming accustomed to his presence for, reassuringly, she had ceased retracting defensively into the settee like a cornered animal and was now looking at him and the room with curiosity.

There were three sharp raps on the door. His sister stood at the front door holding a cloth bag stuffed with clothes. He had made up his mind to not say anything about his predicament for now and after greeting her took the bag and was about to close the door with a cursory thank you when she pressed her hand against it.

'You're not going to just send me off without inviting me in – even for five minutes?' she said.

Reluctantly, he relaxed his grip on the door and replied, 'Come in.'

She smiled complacently – she knew he would find it difficult to refuse her – and walked in ahead of him, darting her head intrusively from side to side to see what might be observable as she passed each doorway down the hall. She stopped, turned to him briskly and asked, 'Now what's all this about a woman friend whose house burnt down and has lost everything? And where is she?'

That was the only thing he could think of on the spur of the moment to satisfy her curiosity when he had asked for women's clothes over the phone.

He fumbled for a response as she fixed her face on him with its sharp blue eyes, aquiline nose and an alertness whose combination always reminded him of a bird, before continuing, 'Now, Laurie, apart from our relations and maybe one or two indifferent female acquaintances, I have never in my life seen you with a woman friend, so don't lie to me! What's this really all about?'

What she said was perfectly true. Laurie had never had an intimate woman friend. He tried to answer but checked himself every time he imaginatively anticipated what he would actually utter and how unbelievably crazy it would sound.

As he hesitated, her eyes bore into him inquisitively and, pursing her lips decisively, she said, 'Laurie, if you're in some kind of trouble, you can tell me, whatever it is. You're my brother and I love you. Blood is thicker than water!'

He knew the very idea that there was a woman in his study in his dressing gown would set off alarm bells in his sister's head. She would imagine all sorts of seedy implications and assume that someone such as she thought him to be, inept in worldly matters, was a potential victim in need of rescue from the clutches of a shameless seductress. In his confusion, he didn't have the wherewithal to justify himself or even the energy to resist and so acquiesced. 'Okay, Rosanna, come this way.'

He led her to the study and, standing at the doorway, extended his arm invitingly for her to enter. He closed his eyes and bit his lip with dread as he anticipated the inevitable response of shock or indignation that would eventuate. The sound of her resolute footsteps on the floorboards ceased; they were followed by something of a huff far short of the gasp he expected.

He waited.

'So what's this all about then? Where is she?'

He stepped in and saw the woman still seated on the settee. She had pulled up her legs, braced her arms around them and buried her face between her knees in a foetal position with fright at the entrance of this stranger.

'There,' he pointed. 'Can't you see her?'

Rosanna exhaled petulantly and said, 'Laurie, if this is your idea of a joke, I'm not amused!'

'There!' he reaffirmed.

'What? A dressing gown heaped up on your settee? Really!'

'But I tell you…' he began but thought better of it and stopped. 'Excuse my little joke, it was in bad taste. I knew you wouldn't believe me and so it was my way of showing you there's no one here. Actually, she's, um, with a friend and I'm going to take the clothes there.'

'A friend, hmm! You have friends? I don't recall ever meeting any of them!' she jeered exasperatedly.

Laurie stood helplessly before this spectacle, curiously turning his head at the woman he could clearly see on the settee and then back to his irritated sister. He made a conscious effort to put his bewilderment aside and would consider this strange inconsistency in a calmer moment when he had the necessary peace to think it through.

'Well, I see I'm not going to get any sense out of you, so I'm leaving. But since there's no one here, you won't be needing these,' she said irascibly, reaching for the bag of clothes in Laurie's hand.

'No!' he cried, retracting the bundle tightly to his chest. In doing so, he saw Rosanna's surprise at his unusually voluble noncompliance and noted too the woman shudder at the pitch of his raised voice.

'All right, you keep them, but tell me, what do you really want those clothes for?'

'As I said, they're for a friend – but not a close one, an acquaintance actually,' he said hoping to allay any misgivings she might have by using a word consistent with her knowledge of his lack of feminine intimates.

She squinted sceptically and said, 'Okay, you have it your way, but I must say a confirmed bachelor who suddenly wants a jumble of women's clothes is odd, if you ask me. I just hope there's nothing funny going on.' She said this with a hint of concern perhaps suggestive that they might be intended for some perverse purpose he couldn't easily admit.

He winced at the very imputation, if that's what she had meant.

As she made her way to the front door, she rattled off a stream of well-meaning advice to which he dutifully nodded.

'If they are for a woman, those clothes, she won't be too keen on wearing another woman's underwear, so I packed some fresh things I bought on the way. They're all there, still in plastic! You men might be indifferent to such matters but a woman, never! No, there's no need for that,' she said as he went to pull out his wallet. 'What do you take me for? You keep your money, I don't want it. I only wish you had the good sense to trust me, that's all I want from you! If you need any help with anything, and I mean anything, you just call, and always remember –'

'Blood is thicker than water,' he interrupted.

She sighed with annoyance at what she took to be his glib interjection. 'My,' she retaliated, 'we are certain of ourselves, aren't we!' She opened the front door and said, 'It's lucky for you, you have a real friend you can depend on – family, I mean – so you just ask if there's anything I can do. I'll call you tomorrow!' She clasped his arms, pecked him on the cheek affectionately and departed, visibly troubled by what had ensued.

Back in his study, the woman had relaxed with Rosanna's departure and sat there looking at him studiously as he stood perplexed in the middle of the room. He wondered why his sister had not been able to see her. Perhaps he was going mad and hallucinating all this. But she was so real and to all intents and purposes absolutely there. He knew he could walk up to her and touch her and she would have the palpability of any mortal; and yet reason told him that it just couldn't be that something real, something in the world, could only be perceived by him and not his sister too, in which case, he had a problem and needed to see someone quickly before it got any worse. He would collect his thoughts, have a precise narrative of everything that had happened sorted out in his mind and see a doctor tomorrow – first thing. For now, he would do his best to ignore the woman, yes, just that, and carry on as usual. It would be difficult with those inscrutable eyes of hers fixed on his every move but he would tell himself it was nothing, a fiction, and pretend she wasn't there.

He tossed aside the bag of clothes. 'You're not there!' he addressed her resolutely.

The woman cocked her head from side to side as a dog might do to glean the meaning of a human utterance addressed to it. She struggled to force herself up and stood uneasily on her feet. After steadying herself, she began shuffling towards him with slow, uncertain steps, and some way towards him stumbled and would have fallen to the floor had he not leapt over and caught her before she could hurt herself. As he cradled her supportively on bended knee, she gazed up at him, initially startled by the unexpected turn of events but quickly yielding him a look of trust as she lay without resistance in his arms. He couldn't ignore her.

Laurie had ten months of long service and annual leave accrued. He took it at half pay and that gave him well over a year and a half of leave. As he had some savings and his needs were modest, he could comfortably manage to support himself for that period. He felt relieved he had a legitimate, if unusual, reason to justify to himself the time taken off and knew he would not miss his work or colleagues, just as they too would not miss him.

During that time, he and his guest became constant companions. He set about educating her as best he could and was frequently amazed by her precocity. She only needed to be shown something once, rarely a few times, before she grasped a concept and applied it unerringly to any comparably new experience. This phenomenon was particularly surprising for Laurie because that sagacious side of her character was amply counterbalanced by a naivety as pronounced. This was to be expected, he surmised, and would probably diminish over time as she garnered a greater store of personal experience. However, this kind of duality seemed to permeate all aspects of her character. She would, for instance, at times remain withdrawn, even aloof, and then at others snuggle up to him on the couch like a child, using his foreleg as a pillow as she drifted off cozily to sleep.

Early on in this venture, when she had started to speak coherently, he tried to discover if she had a name but none was forthcoming. He asked her what she would like to be called and she looked at him blankly. He could not go on referring to her as just his 'guest' or 'the woman', he told her, and so suggested a number of names he thought reflected her mysterious beauty. He ran through a list of them and she stopped him on Laylah, asking, 'That has a nice sound. What does it mean?'

'As far as I'm aware, it's the Arabic for "night" and to my mind it does go well with those deep dark eyes of yours.'

She smiled and nodded.

'Laylah it is then!' he smiled back.

Each day, he would spend some hours reading to her. As she had an excellent memory, her vocabulary expanded rapidly and it wasn't too long before she was able to read to him. He loved to sit back, close his eyes and listen to the perfect diction and beautifully paced phrasing with which she delivered a reading in that low and sublimely melodious voice of hers. At the end of a session, he would return from his transport, look at her admiringly and clap softly in token of the superlative effort that had brought him so much pleasure.

The literature they shared was diverse, anything from Sappho to T.S. Eliot, Seneca to Jung, or Plato to Nietzsche. Plato in particular held a fascination for her and she engaged with the texts available with such perspicacity that Laurie was often left marvelling at the trains of logic she elicited and which he had never considered in comparable depth despite his many years of interest in that thinker. There were also times when she made brazen assertions as if she had direct access to realities denied others. As far as she was concerned, the absolute objectivity of Plato's ideas was self-evident. She might say, for instance, there was a certain point at which reason must falter in its finite applicability of principles and no sophistication of argumentation could demonstrate the platonic ideas unless one were capable, as Plato himself perhaps was, of elevating oneself to that contemplative level of reality. That presupposed not only the laborious perfecting of intellect but also a sublimation of the total strata of one's spiritual being. Words were imprecise, that was clear, but they could never be understood at all if they were not underpinned by something inviolable, an essence, that made their approximations valid or even merely serviceable.

'No amount of accurate description or definition of the colour red can make it accessible to anyone who is colour-blind and cannot apprehend it for himself, and that is the same with platonic ideas,' she once said, going on to say enigmatically with eyes at once downcast and perhaps rueful, 'Essence is existence as I know it but that's not the case for you because you have a will that limits possibility to choice. I don't...'

In his puzzlement, Laurie asked, 'What exactly does that mean?'

She sighed thoughtfully and responded, 'That I am eternal, and it is I who will, one day, be nursing you…'

There was something troubling in that comment that flabbergasted him but which he set aside, uncertain as to its import or how to respond.

Besides the foregoing subjects, he taught her geography and media studies, good he thought for acclimatising her to her worldly context, and the lower end of intermediate numeracy, a skill he was not brilliant at. But even there, she had the capacity to build on the rudimentary knowledge he was able to teach so that she could go on to apply it to mathematical operations more advanced than he could understand. When she tried explaining them to him, he would plainly admit he had no comprehension of what she was saying.

'But it's easy. Come on, you can do it,' she would coax him earnestly, upon which he would shake his head and stroke her shoulder affectionately as he guffawed at his ineptitude.

Something of this strange combination of precocity and naivety was discernible the first time she caught her reflection in a mirror. She screamed with fright and when Laurie asked her what the matter was, she told him there was a woman in the house spying on her. When Laurie realised what had happened, he overcame her fearful reluctance and got her to stand before the mirror.

'That's a reflection of you,' he told her. 'See, I'm reflected in it too. The surface of the mirror is so finely polished and smooth that it reflects light, like still water does. You must have noticed that. Now, since the light has carried off our images in the first place, the mirror bounces back that light and we see ourselves as images – that's the best I can do to explain it, I'm afraid…'

She extended a hand and attempted to touch her reflected face but only felt the cold surface of glass and saw that the image of her face remained removed from the intended point of tactility. As she did so, she saw too, to her puzzlement, her hand similarly reflected and, where one finger appeared to touch another, there was no sensation of bodily contact with warm, soft flesh but a tactility, altogether baffling, of unyielding hardness. She withdrew her hand and tested again. After a moment, she alternated inquisitively between looking at Laurie and his reflection, comparing the two impressions. For some time, she stood there fascinated by her image, moving her hand or face to see if there were any inconsistency between the motion she intended and the behaviour of her reflection.

After that experience, she found an old science textbook from Laurie's schooldays and devoured the section on optics. One day while she stood before a mirror, she said to him, 'You can't see my image in the mirror from where you're standing.'

Laurie, surprised by the unexpected comment, looked up and replied, 'Yes, that's right. How do you come to that conclusion?'

'Because I can't see yours, which means that we, as the object locations of our reflected images, are not situated within the range of a shared normal line of sight, that being the perpendicular relative to an incident ray and its reflected ray. Hence the image locations of our reflections are not visible to each other. For that, we would require a larger reflective plane and this mirror is too small for that. Or, to put it simply, as the angle of incidence must equal the angle of reflection, were your eyes visible to me, I would know that by retracing the reflected ray I see back to its point of incidence, it would fold back correspondingly to your line of sight, and therefore my reflected image would be visible to you.'

'Oh,' he said, nonplussed.

Mirrors didn't trouble her after that.

Laurie had never felt so happy. He had initially feared his relationship to Laylah would be an encroachment on his independence, a burden, but contrary to that expectation felt contented and eager to return home whenever he had some errand to attend to, such as shopping or bills to pay at the post office. He often caught himself wondering why he had never realised just how barren and lonely his existence before her arrival had been.

He even felt like a doting parent, especially when they went on excursions to broaden her view of the world. Their first took place when he introduced her to his backyard. It was a brilliant, sunny day when she stood outside the confines of the house for the first time, at which point her face took on a look of exultation. Shielding her eyes, she gazed up at the sparsely clouded sky and pointed at them with speechless wonder. Then she looked about her in something of a disorientated stupor, overwhelmed by the mélange of new impressions. The purple inflorescences of the lush salvias growing by the fence caught her eye. She approached them curiously and ran a hand over the leaves and then the flower heads, pausing to rub the petals between her fingers.

A bee lit on one and in her fascination she was about to touch it when Laurie pulled her hand back and said, 'No don't do that. You'll get stung and that hurts!'

She looked at him with puzzlement, not knowing what he meant.

Before he could explain, she gasped with pleasure and traced the wavy aerial movement of a cabbage moth with her finger; then, running after it like an excited child, she stooped to observe it as it wafted from flower to flower. Laurie watched with delight, smiling as she went from tree to plant, lawn to rock, object to object running explorative hands over them and giggling with pleasure at each new sensation or wrinkling her brow with curiosity. It struck him as strange that when they read to each other, it seemed as if she had definite pictures of these things based on what he had told her, but clearly that was not exactly the case. When she experienced something directly for the first time, he could see a look of revelation sweep over her face as she connected an actual thing with the idea or word that represented it.

There was a park nearby and Laurie made it a daily ritual to walk there together. There they would take in the sights, exchange thoughts on subjects of interest or, like close friends who feel no discomfort in prolonged silence, simply walk sedately arm in arm. This pastime had been the cause of some perturbation for Laurie initially because he tended to forget that others couldn't see Laylah and a solitary man gesticulating expressively to no one in particular and apparently talking to himself did raise an eyebrow or two.

After he became aware of the queer looks people had been giving him and their cautious avoidance of him as they approached one another on the path, he decided on a ruse. He got himself an earpiece, stuck it in a phone and pretended he was conversing by those means whenever he was out with Laylah. That seemed to allay any unwanted interest in him but some habitués of the park did nonetheless wonder why he kept his left arm crooked in that peculiar way.

At times, Laurie still felt disturbed that no one else could see Laylah. After all, it wasn't as if she behaved like a hallucination. There was in their shared experience a consistency in no way capricious, at once predictably stable and evolving organically. She did not, for instance, pop in and out of existence. She seemed to sense this troubled feeling in him and maybe out of a kind of automatic sympathy, for she often reflected his moods or, because of a need growing out of her worldly becoming, once hinted at something that made Laurie wonder if she too felt constricted by her invisibility. She had by then seen many people and he asked himself if, based on her experiences with him, ones altogether of consideration and tender regard, she felt some disappointment for her inability to share with others of his kind similar experiences which she, in all probability, assumed would be equally satisfying.

Laurie was all too conscious that he was the only other being in her life and that she, in her dependence on him, frequently followed him around in expectation of what they might do together. Even though he had fitted her out with a room, she would tiptoe to his at night like a frightened child and creep into his bed. At first he was discomforted by those visits and would have preferred she kept to herself but in the end accepted them as just another peculiar instance of the unusual relationship he had found himself thrust into with this enigmatic being.

In an attempt to encourage some independence in her, which he would build up by stages, he suggested she go out and walk to the corner shop and back on her own, or even just a few houses down the street. She looked at him stunned and shook her head anxiously.

'What's the matter? There's nothing to worry about. It'll be good for you,' he said.

Again, she shook her head emphatically.

'Look, if no one can see you, no one can hurt you.'

In response, her expression flickered between something unnerving he couldn't interpret and one of obvious displeasure as if she were deeply wounded by what he had said. She turned from him sulkily and retreated to her room without a word.

'Laylah, wait!' he cried out after her, troubled he had unwittingly hurt her.

In her room, she lay on her bed looking up at the ceiling and remained unresponsive to his attempts to coax her out of her gloom. Crouching beside the bed to soothe her, his heart nearly snapped when he saw a large luminous tear spill down her rigidly statuesque face.

The next day, everything returned to normal as if nothing had happened, and so things continued. But not long after, as he sat in his study, she entered and stood before him silently. She had a strange expression unlike any he had seen before, one perhaps of conflict between a reticence she was struggling to suppress and firming resolve.

'What's up?' he asked her.

'You have to a allow me to will for myself,' she replied.

'But of course, Laylah, you don't need my permission for that. You're free to do what you like.'

'No, I'm not free…'

'Look, I'll support you any way I can. If you want to walk out of the front door and explore the world for yourself, I won't stop you.'

'I can't do that without a will.'

Laurie leaned back in his chair and cupped his chin reflectively in his hand. 'But what am I supposed to do if you won't will for yourself? I can't do any more than allow you to do what you want…'

She lowered her head pensively and said, 'You have to will my will…'

'Will your will?' he said perplexedly. 'Laylah, how can I do that? I'm not God.'

'Ideas are real, Laurie and will is no different. Every object in this room began as nothing more than an idea and remains so.'

'And am I just an idea, then?' he smiled.

'You are a will whose essence is desire and that book before you, the table, pens – everything – are what you have desirously willed to possess and even brought into being in your community of wills with others.'

'I'm not sure I understand what you're getting at, but that is an extreme view of will, Laylah, a level of freedom I'm not sure I accept, want to accept. I mean, that makes me and my so-called community of wills responsible for everything, even desires we may not recognise we have or would actually want to fulfil.'

'That's no reason why you can't will into being what you unconsciously desire.'

'That's a rather ethically austere notion in its implications. I don't know what to say…'

In the ensuing silence, Laylah lowered her head glumly, disappointed by his incomprehension and turned to go.

'Hang on,' Laurie appealed.

She turned to face him.

'So what would you have me do?' he asked.

'You must imagine me with a will of my own and tell yourself that in your thoughts. Concentrate with real effort and direct that idea to me.'

Laurie sighed quietly and said, 'I'm not sure if it'll help but okay, for you, Laylah, I'll do it.'

She immediately brightened up, went and crouched beside him and asked cheerfully whether they would read to each other later as he bemusedly scratched his chin.

Laurie felt decidedly silly attempting to perform what Laylah had requested. The times he half-heartedly did so, he couldn't help succumbing to the feeling of the futility of it all and gave up. He tried to force himself just to be true to his word but lapsed into periods of in-activity after each attempt.

That was until about a month after when Laylah told him, 'You're not really trying.'

'How do you know that?' he said evasively.

'Because I know when you do – I can feel it.'

'You know?' he responded sceptically.

She pressed her lips knowingly and nodded.

'But how could you?'

'On the Thursday after my request, which was a Wednesday four weeks ago, if you remember, you did it for about five minutes. Then the following night, Friday, you did it again but stopped abruptly until three days later, Monday that was, and since then you've kept stopping and starting with long gaps so that as soon as I feel an inner resolve forming, it leaches away again. Would you like the exact dates since our agreement if you don't believe me? I've kept a record.'

'You've kept a… No, no, no need, what you say rings true, perfectly true, I believe you,' Laurie replied, reflecting in a funk. 'You actually know when I –? That's astounding! Okay, you've convinced me. Rest assured I'll dedicate myself to our project.'

Laurie set a time every night when he devoted himself to projecting his will, as he came to call it, towards Laylah. He concentrated on keeping a picture of her in mind while imagining the idea of his will radi-ating out and transferring its force to her. Some nights, he would feel quite innervated from his efforts. Strangely, the more he did this, the stronger her confidence grew. She said to him on one occasion that she would prove that his sincere and regular efforts were working by going down the street on her own, which she did.

One night while Laurie sat at his desk and Laylah lay curled asleep on the settee in his study, he was projecting his will when he noticed a glint in the glass before him. It was nothing more than the light re-flected from the desk lamp but when he moved his head, he saw a play of spectral colours. He got so fascinated by this that, in his fixation on it, entered something of a trance while some other part of his mind continued concentrating on Laylah. In that altered state, which must have gone on some considerable time, it seemed to Laurie he could hear a distant voice increasing in intensity saying, 'I can feel it. I can feel it.' He snapped out of his trance, drenched in sweat, and saw Laylah smiling in her sleep muttering, 'I can feel it!'

He slumped in his chair exhausted and in the same moment Laylah opened her eyes with a look of astonishment.

She got up off the settee and went to him. 'Thank you,' she said, as she bent over him and kissed him affectionately on the cheek. She had never done that before.

Laurie sat disoriented, overwhelmed as much by that spontaneous act of tenderness as the unwitting hypnotic state he had self-induced and the lingering haziness resulting from it.

After that fateful night, everything changed. Laylah became more independent, even autonomous in certain respects. Eschewing her former coyness, she began initiating activities they might do together. On one memorable day, she said, 'I want to go for a stroll in the park. Let's go!'

Laurie, at once agreeable to the idea and yet surprised by the commanding tone in which it was delivered, acquiesced bemusedly.

But if that were not of itself remarkable, what happened later left him speechless. As usual, they ambled along in the park in their leisurely way with Laurie hooked into his phone. While they talked, a girl of about nine played with a ball immediately before them when she fumbled and it rolled over to Laylah's foot. The girl ran over to collect it but before she could, Laylah picked it up and held it out to her.

The girl, surprised by that unexpected proffering of her ball, looked at Laylah, whom she obviously found unusually striking, with something approaching awe. She took the ball, nodded shyly and said, 'Thank you.'

Laurie shook his head involuntarily with surprise while the girl stood transfixed on Laylah. He broke her spell when, pointing to Laylah, he asked the girl, 'My friend here, you can see her?'

The girl creased her brow incomprehensibly as if to indicate the irrelevance of his question and replied, 'Yes.'

Before she could go, he added, 'And what does she look like?'

'Well, she has long black hair, very white skin, a lovely nose like my auntie Sophie's – no, nicer – and big, dark beautiful eyes.'

'And what's she wearing?'

'That's silly, mister. Everyone can see it's a dress with different coloured flowers on it...'

'Amy, come here right now!' a woman shouted to the girl.

Amy took her leave with a smile to Laylah, a sceptical look at Laurie, and skipped off happily to two women who were sitting on a bench talking.

As Laurie and Laylah began walking, he could hear one of the women saying to Amy, 'How many times have I told you not to talk to strangers, especially men.'

'But it's not just a man, mum, there's a beautiful woman there with him,' Amy responded.

'A woman – where?'

'There beside him,' Amy pointed.

'I can't see any woman,' her mum said before her companion interjected, 'Yes, there she is, see?'

'Oh yes,' the mother responded, 'so there is... Anyway, don't talk to strangers...'

Laurie's head was in a whirl and his heart pounded with excitement. So others could see her too! She was real, as he had always known her to be, and now he had independent confirmation of it.

Laylah felt his excitement and, placing her head affectionately on his shoulder, said, 'It's all because of you, Laurie. You freed me.'

It became increasingly clear to Laurie that what had passed was not an isolated incident. Laylah had, quite inexplicably, become a being as worldly as any of flesh and blood. Elated as he was by this turn of events, there was nonetheless for some time afterwards a sense of unreality to it unlike any he had experienced since their meeting, particularly when he heard people making complimentary remarks about 'that intriguing woman' on his arm.

Laurie got tired of seeing Laylah in his sister's clothes. He suggested they go out and do some shopping. That was not his sort of thing at all and yet there was something altogether pleasing about it. He felt a warm glow when Laylah emerged from the changing booth and paraded before him, her gaze looking for the slightest sign that suggested pleasure or approval in what he saw. One item in particular had mutual appeal. It was a black dress that tapered to her knees and hugged her body so that its splendidly feminine rhythms were beautifully pronounced. Twirling before him from side to side as she ran her hands over her hips, she saw him nodding to himself with a wistful smile and without hesitation said, 'I'll take this one!'

From there, they went and bought some jewellery.

They were on their way home from another pleasant walk in the park when Laurie heard his name called from a distance. His heart sank when he saw Barry hurriedly making his way over. Laylah noticed the tensing of his jaw and asked him what was wrong. He muttered something barely audible about differences that puzzled her because Barry, upon stepping up to them, extended a firm and genial hand, to which Laurie limply reciprocated.

'Well, what a surprise! We've often speculated what you've been up to all these months.' Then turning to Laylah with obvious fascination, he said as he extended his hand, 'I see you haven't been wasting your time. Hello, I'm Barry.'

'Laylah,' she replied.

'A beautiful name,' he said in lingering entrancement so that Laylah had to forcibly withdraw her hand from his. 'Laurie, you never let on you keep such interesting company.' Then sizing up the marked difference in ages between them, he added, 'Is this a relative of yours, a niece perhaps?'

'We're friends.' interjected Laylah.

'Friends? Oh…and you live around here?'

'Not long but yes – I live with Laurie.'

He turned to Laurie with bafflement, 'But how did you…?'

The look of disbelief on Barry's face was patent. Why someone as extraordinarily beautiful, and young, as Laylah would companion someone as drab and middle-aged as Laurie was beyond his comprehension. Laylah noticed this and was taken aback by his reaction. Laurie registered her surprise and in his growing unease feared that this handsome man's interest in her might inspire the idea that there was something questionable, or even deficient, in their relationship.

Barry interposed himself between them and said, 'Well, if you ever need someone, a friend, to show you around the traps, it'd be my pleasure.'

Laylah looked past him, gestured him aside with a gentle motion of her hand and sidled up to Laurie, crooking her arm in his.

'Thank you, but Laurie is the only friend I need. We'd better get a move on if we still want to see that exhibition.' She nodded indifferently to Barry and led Laurie off in her arm.

The look of stupefaction on Barry's face filled Laurie with delight. For once, Barry had got the comeuppance he deserved and he, Laurie, was not only there to witness it but could even in some measure pride himself on being, however indirectly, an essential part of it. He braced Laylah's arm tighter in his and felt her happily reciprocate, much as lovers do when they press ever harder against each other as they strive to approach the spiritual centre of a love to which even their bodies are an obstacle.

As they walked on, Laylah cast a glance backwards to see Barry slowly pacing after them with dumfounded hesitation. Upon seeing her looking at him, he stopped, looked away and began walking in another direction.

For some time, Laurie felt that Laylah was growing restless, troubled for some reason he couldn't fathom. She would look at him strangely and he often caught her staring at him with something of a brooding fascination. When he asked her why she was staring, she would shrug with apparent incomprehension or mutter elusive responses he couldn't decipher. Should he press her at such moments, his inability to understand her only succeeded in irritating her and frequently provoked curt replies he didn't know how to interpret.

When he thought about the way she looked at him, it seemed as if she were somehow pleading to him for something. There was sadness in that look and maybe even an unspoken distress of some kind. He grew worried about her and made up his mind to get to the bottom of it.

The next time he encountered that state of gloomy fascination, he spoke up. 'Laylah, I'm a little concerned. Tell me, is something upsetting you?'

She shook her head briskly with averted eyes.

'Now I can see there is! You know I can't help you if you don't open up...'

'There's nothing, nothing!'

'Laylah, dear, why have you stopped trusting me?'

She remained rigid with fear as the tears she was struggling to hold back welled in her eyes. Laurie, moved by her anguish, clasped her affectionately, upon which she laid her head on his shoulder and quietly sobbed.

'There, there,' he said stroking her hair, 'there's nothing so bad that we can't work out...'

'I'm scared...' she sniffled.

'Scared – of what?'

After a pause in which she seemed to be undergoing an inner tug 'o war to say what was bothering her, she whispered, 'Feelings...'

'Feelings?' muttered Laurie quizzically as he continued stroking her hair.

She drew back slightly and looked at him with that pleading look that had so troubled him of late.

'Go on, Laylah, tell me more...'

With her head bowed and her bottom lip quivering, she said, 'When we...when we go out...in the park, I...I see them...'

'See who?'

'Lovers... I see them walking hand in hand or lying together and kissing and I wonder what it's like... I want to know what it's like...'

'Oh, I see!' Laurie said, nonplussed.

She raised her eyes slowly to him and only then did he realise the significance of the look that had so baffled him. It was a look of yearning, a profound and painful yearning uncertain how to find fulfilment or, in her case, even make sense of itself and appealing to him for help.

'Will you show me?' she asked.

Laurie was speechless and stood with his mouth agape trying to find the words with which to respond.,'I… I don't know what to…'

While he fumbled, Laylah clasped his face impetuously and smacked an artless kiss on his lips. She pulled back awkwardly and scrutinised him attentively. 'Is that how it's done?' she asked.

In his bewilderment, Laurie hesitated from responding. Seeing her attempt did not have the effect she had observed, or expected, she slapped a barrage of inelegant and indefinite kisses on his terrified face.

He gently clasped her hands and drew her back. 'Laylah, no, I can't… I…can't…

'But you've taught me everything…' she said. 'I need to know…'

'This is different, Laylah. Look, you may not understand this but you're like a daughter to me…and even if it wasn't like that, I'm not… I couldn't anyway…'

Laylah withdrew her hands from Laurie's and dropped her head despondently. They stood there uncomfortably until she muttered, 'I've made a fool of myself, haven't I?'

'No! No, just surprised me, that's all. But Laylah, you've always surprised me and that's something I love about you,' Laurie said magnanimously to spare her embarrassment.

She looked at him dejectedly and, crushed by feelings of rejection, strange and overwhelming to her, turned and left the room without another word. He wanted to call out after her but, just as if he were in a dream, froze impotently with each attempt to make a sound.

It troubled Laurie deeply that Laylah began avoiding him. She disappeared at night and when he'd ask her about what she'd done on her nocturnal excursions, she averted her eyes and said she just felt like being alone. He would wait up, fretting until he heard the front door creak open and knew she was back and safe at home. Often, he fell asleep at his desk and would not see her the following day while she sequestered herself in her room until her next outing. All the while, he felt himself grow weary, hopelessly weary, and paralysed by an inability to erase the distance he felt had grown between them. Worse than anything, he feared she no longer needed him…

Laurie had, of course, kept in touch with his sister – he had no choice – but in those exchanges with her avoided any reference to the mysterious acquaintance for whom he had once sought clothes. Lately, though, his sister had become worried. Do what she might, she got no reply from him when she called and so decided on an impromptu visit.

She knocked and knocked at his door but got no response. As she did so with increasing vehemence, the door creaked open. That surprised her. Laurie would never leave it unlocked. A feeling of foreboding came over her as she walked in cautiously calling out his name. She was appalled by the fetid smell and disarray before her. There were piles of dirty laundry and what appeared to be full bags of shopping rotting in the hall. Laurie was a man of scrupulous habits when it came to cleanliness and order so she knew something was terribly wrong. In a panic, her pace quickened and she headed to the lounge room.

There he lay on the couch looking visibly aged, his wrinkled and sallow skin drawn over his cadaverous face. Overcome with horror at his plight, she ran over and crouched beside him. Try as she might to rouse him, he was prey to a lassitude so profound he only responded with difficulty.

'Oh, Laurie, love, what's wrong?' she pleaded.

He raised a feeble hand and whispered hoarsely, 'Thirsty, water… water…'

She went to the kitchen and was again disgusted by the pervasive squalor. The sink, filled with stagnant grey water, had putrid blobs of matter floating on it and unwashed plates lay stacked about in higgledy-piggledy piles stopped only from toppling over, it seemed, by the congealed food holding them fast. Startled by the sudden movement of mice as they gleefully foraged about the rich pickings, she screamed as they scurried off at her disturbance.

She found a clean glass, filled it with water and returned to Laurie. Holding his head tenderly, she brought it to his lips. He drank it greedily. Just then, she heard the sound of footfalls approaching down the hall. She turned to see Laylah, cigarette in hand, enter, stop and look at her with haughty nonchalance.

Rosanna looked at Laurie inquisitively and then at the stranger. Laylah had had her long hair cut in a fashionably asymmetrical bobbed style. She wore blood-red lipstick, eyeshadow and thick mascara. Rosanna thought it all overdone. With her large ebony eyes receding into these shadowing effects, it made them seem at times as if there were two craters where eyes should be. Those touches, along with her short, tight black skirt and leather boots surmounting her knees, the belted leopard chiffon blouse, square-cut hip-length leather jacket and shoulder bag made her look severely imposing.

'And who might you be?' Rosanna asked apprehensively.

'I could very well ask you the same question. I happen to live here,' Laylah said as she drew on her cigarette pertly. Ignoring Rosanna, she stepped before the window, looked at her muted reflection and, turning her face from side to side, adjusted an earring.

'But, of course, I do remember you,' Laylah said with her back to Rosanna. 'We have been acquainted. You're Laurie's sister.'

'Don't be ridiculous. We've never met. I'd be bound to remember anyone as…well, like you!' Rosanna said.

Laylah smirked sardonically and said, 'Well, that just goes to show how feeble-mindedness runs in the family.'

'Laurie, are you going to let her talk to us like that?' Rosanna cried indignantly.

Laurie waved his hand irresolutely.

Laylah turned towards them and began rummaging in her bag. 'Money, I need money,' she said petulantly. She went to the coffee table adjacent to where Laurie lay and picked up his wallet. She opened it and took what was there. 'This'll do for now but I need more, you hear? I need more!' she said irritably to Laurie.

'You can't do that! How dare you – give that back!' Rosanna leapt up protectively of her brother, attempting to wrest the money out of Laylah's hands.

'It's mine!' Laylah growled, delivering a firm smack on her cheek with the back of her hand.

Rosanna reeled back with the unexpected force of the blow and fell to the floor, clasping her face painfully. Incensed, she got to her feet and prepared to lunge at Laylah to return in kind what she had received.

Before she could follow through, Laylah said coolly, 'Laurie, tell this sister of yours to know her place. She has no right to come between us.'

Raising his hand feebly, he gestured to Rosanna to desist. He strained, turned on his side and leaned over to the coffee table. With difficulty he scrawled the password to his bank account on a piece of paper. 'Here, the password,' he whispered breathlessly. 'You can take as much as you need. My card is in my wallet…'

Laylah smiled smugly at Rosanna. She removed the credit card from the wallet, snatched up the paper and deposited them in her bag. Rosanna glowered at what she took to be nothing short of insolence and in her concern for Laurie kneeled beside him.

'Laurie, dear, I don't think you know what you're doing! You can't just let this…this…you can't just let anyone do as they please with your money. Laurie, please, you've got to come to your senses.'

In his innervated state, the wrangling between the two women seemed to further tax him beyond endurance. Hopelessly divided in himself, he stared indecisively and in his growing anguish put his hands to his face and cried, 'Stop! Stop it!'

Laylah went to the bar, stubbed her cigarette out on it and poured herself a neat Scotch. She turned, leaned against the bar and studied the scene before her with clinical detachment. 'See, you're upsetting him!' she said, downing the Scotch. She poured herself another.

'Laurie, dear, I'm going to get you out of here. Come on, come with me.'

'You can't do that. Where he goes I go,' Laylah said with a smirk.

'Not likely! Come on, Laurie, just put your arm around my shoulder…'

'He's not going anywhere, are you, Laurie?'

Laurie shook his head obediently.

'Well, I can't leave you like this. I'm going to get help. The police, I'm going to call the police…'

'You do that and we'll both have you out on your ear for trespassing, won't we, Laurie?'

Laurie nodded.

'In fact, I might even call the police myself if you don't stop making a nuisance of yourself. But for now I have more important things to do.' She downed the Scotch and thumped the glass on the bar. She walked over to Laurie, ran her hand superciliously through his hair and said, 'I won't be back till late. Don't wait up.'

Laurie mumbled something inaudible.

Laylah turned to leave and Rosanna rose and followed her down the hall screaming, 'I don't know who you think you are but I won't stand for it! If you think you can do as you please round here, you're mistaken! There'll be trouble, you hear! Trouble!'

Unruffled by Rosanna's outburst, Laylah turned at the front door and said, 'Yes, there will be trouble but you'll bear the brunt of it. I don't expect to find you in my house when I get back.' She slammed the door in Rosanna's face.

Rosanna remained immobile, stunned by what had passed. For a moment, she was uncertain what to do but her native decisiveness quickly returned and she hurried back to Laurie. 'I'm going to call a doctor. You look terrible,' she said.

'No need, I was just a bit off colour but I'm coming back to myself' he protested.

Strangely enough, when Rosanna took a closer look at him, he did seem suddenly better, certainly nothing like the emaciated man of some moments ago. His voice too had reclaimed something of its usual timbre. As he had no wish to see a doctor and said so with increasing firmness, Rosanna desisted.

She was, however, adamant in her attempts to get him to cut himself loose of Laylah. It was clear to her that woman was not good for him and had to be given the shove. Laurie would hear nothing of it and told Rosanna the spiritual bond between them was unbreakable. Rosanna had to hold herself back from wryly interjecting that she saw well enough the quality of that 'spiritual bond' in the contemptuous way she had treated him.

Try as she might, he remained immovable but, she thought with a glimmer of hopeful scepticism, perhaps not indefinitely so. She sensed that while he outwardly held firm in his loyalty to Laylah, there was at some deeper level a hesitant, counter-intent to be free of her but which he somehow didn't have the capacity or strength of will to admit to himself. She would try again later but didn't want to exacerbate the inner turmoil this subject no doubt caused him. She told him to relax and set about putting the house in order.

Within a few hours, she had it spick and span and even cobbled together a hearty lentil and vegetable soup with what was still usable.

Laurie sat on the couch abstractedly staring into space when she entered with a bowl of steaming soup.

She placed it on the table and set a chair facing him. 'Here, have some of this,' she said, about to start spooning it to him.

'That's not necessary, Roz. I'm not an invalid, I can feed myself.' He took the bowl, set it on his lap and began eating. He was clearly famished. 'It's good. You haven't lost your touch.'

'I'm happy to come here any time and cook you a healthy meal.'

'No need. You didn't have to clean up either, I would have got around to it, but thanks. It's appreciated…'

'Laurie, dear, I don't want to harp on things that upset you but tell me, how did you get into this mess?'

'What mess?'

'That horrible woman! I can see she's not interested in anything but herself.'

'Don't talk that way about her. You don't understand.'

'Oh, I think I do. You're an ageing, lonely man who's been duped by a gold digger out to suck you dry of everything you've got.'

'I told you, don't speak about her like that.'

'It's really not worth it, Laurie, whatever, well, little favours she might grant.'

'It's not like you think.'

'Well, tell me then…'

'You wouldn't believe me even if I could.'

'You could at least try…'

'Look, she's not really like what you saw today. That wasn't her. She's just a little lost, confused, at the moment, that's all. She'll come back to herself and then you'll see.'

'She's not the one who's confused,' Rosanna sighed disconsolately to herself.

While Laurie ate, she sat before him with a host of questions whirling in her head she wanted to ask but which she knew would not be answered. She was now at a loss for what to do and knew there wouldn't be any cooperation from him.

'I think you should go, Roz.'

'Are you sure now you want me to go?'

'Yes, it's best.'

'Okay, but I'm coming back tomorrow and regularly from now on to see how you're going. I have that spare key you gave me.'

'You can only come if you promise to not upset Laylah.'

'Not upset Laylah? Laurie, she struck me for God's sake!' she gasped indignantly.

'I don't want to be caught up in a tug o' war between two angry women. My nerves won't take it.'

'Laurie, what is this obsession you have with that…that…well, there's no other word for it – bitch?'

Laurie thumped the empty bowl on the table and growled, 'I won't say it again, don't speak of her disrespectfully.'

'Okay, okay,' Rosanna responded, shocked by his vehemence. She shook her head incredulously, put up her hands and said, 'I'm going… I'm going.' She took the bowl and returned with another serve of soup and a jug of water which she set on the table beside the glass. 'You're obviously hungry so, here, have another bowl.'

'Thanks, Roz.'

'I'll see you tomorrow and I promise I'll be on my best behaviour,' she said with bitter irony, before concluding, 'And Laurie, whatever happens, always remember, "Blood is thicker than water."'

When he heard the front door close, Laurie sighed with relief that he was finally alone. This longing for solitude was something he increasingly felt of late. Whenever Laylah departed, he would feel reinvigorated and recover the capacity for long-standing interests he had neglected, though not without intermittently fretting for her.

He was still seated on the lounge absorbed in one of his favourite books when the clock struck two a.m. The stillness broken by its volume and suddenness startled him, sending shockwaves through his chest and the back of his neck. A feeling of foreboding took possession of him so that his engrossment in the book he held suddenly dispersed. As always when he felt this way, a sudden listlessness debilitated him and he had to lie down. He knew she was close, very close, and felt a mixture of relief for her safety and anguish for the indifference with which she would pass him by on the way to her room without acknowledging him.

The front door opened. He could hear two voices as footsteps traversed the hall, hers and someone else's. He turned his head apprehensively towards the lounge room door when Barry leaned in the doorway with the pronounced biceps on his upraised arm showing over his shortsleeved shirt and his top lip curled contemptuously. He studied Laurie coolly before taking a few paces forward and stopping with a smirk. Laylah followed him and Laurie was dismayed when he saw the disorderly state she was in. As had been the case lately, she was drunk and her dissolute behaviour, extended nightly excursions and little sleep were taking their toll. Her skin had started to lose its once incomparable splendour and dark rings were showing under her eyes. Laylah drew up behind Barry, put her clasped hands on his shoulder and rested her chin on them. They stood there staring at him in unnerving silence.

Laurie flinched helplessly in his distress as he laboured to question the meaning of this intrusion but words failed him.

'Get us a drink, Lay. Would you like one, Laurie?' said Barry.

Laurie remained speechless.

'I suppose not. Just make it two then.'

Laylah passed him a Scotch and sipped on hers as she looked at Laurie coldly.

Making a determined effort, Laurie said, 'What are you doing in my house? Get out!'

Clasping Laylah around the waist, Barry said, 'My girl here invited me in. You wouldn't be so unromantic now as to stand in the way of love, would you?'

Laylah giggled at his sassiness and rubbed her nose affectionately across his cheek.

'Lay here thought it was about time she brought me home so we could get together properly without having to do it on the sly or out of the way places… It's a bit difficult at my place with my partner around…' he added cavalierly.

Laylah smirked in admiration of his brazenness.

Walking about the room and nodding approvingly, he said, 'So this is your place, Lay, not bad…not bad. I might take you up on the offer to move in.'

Laurie began making incomprehensible sounds in his growing agitation which only heightened their amusement. Barry gestured to Laylah with a nod to pay him attention and then crouched beside Laurie. As he addressed him, Barry emphasised his statements by poking Laurie's nose derisively with his index finger, at which Laylah chuckled.

'Your problem is you're unsociable. Know what I mean?'

He put his Scotch on the floor beside him. Here, Barry squeezed Laurie's cheeks in his hand so that his lips pouted ridiculously while he shook his head from side to side. 'What, you don't understand what I mean?' He repeated the grotesque shaking of Laurie's head. Again, he started pressing his nose. 'Well, it's like this, you see, you've got to make an effort and lighten up. Stop being an old stick in the mud. Now do you get me?' He gripped Laurie's face and shook his head in the same manner. 'Nope, he still doesn't get it! Maybe this might help.' He lifted Laurie's head by his hair and poured his Scotch into his mouth.

Much of it spilled over Laurie's face but some trickled down his windpipe and he gasped for breath, coughing convulsively.

'Get me another,' Barry commanded Laylah.

She took his glass and with a roguish grin gave him hers. He poured it down Laurie's throat. By this time, Laurie's face had turned scarlet and tears rolled down his cheeks as he spluttered and choked.

'See, isn't that better? Nah? Aw, this guy's hopeless, no sense of fun,' Barry said as he thrust his head back and patted him on the cheek contemptuously.

Laylah threw her head back, shuddering with laughter.

Barry got up, yawned and stretched with the luxurious languor of someone thoroughly at home. He walked over to Laylah, looked at her thoughtfully and then cast a glance at Laurie, who was still gasping. He clasped her hair, pulled her head back forcefully and gave her a long, lurid kiss to which she greedily responded. Though Laurie's vision was blurry from his coughing fit, he could make them out as they kissed and fondled each other.

Barry removed her leather jacket, turned, aimed, and flung it at Laurie across the room so that it draped over his face. Laurie started at the unexpectedness of it and they laughed. Instinctively shocked by sudden enveloping darkness and feeling as though he were suffocating, he put up his hands feebly to his face and tugged at the jacket until it slid off onto the floor.

'That's perfect,' Barry jeered. 'I want him to see this.'

He gestured to Laylah to remove her blouse. She unfastened her belt, let it drop and took off her blouse. She cast it in Laurie's direction but it fell short of the couch onto the floor.

'That too,' Barry said, flicking the strap of her bra. As Laylah unclipped it, Barry held his upraised palms towards her and said with mocking theatricality, 'Now, what any real, red-blooded man wouldn't want a piece of this?'

Laylah threw her bra at Laurie, upon which Barry commenced devouring her lasciviously. Laurie turned away, buried his face in the couch and whimpered pitiably. All the while, Barry made lewd remarks that induced Laylah to join in gleefully, perversely intoxicated by her power to wound Laurie with every utterance.

Barry lit a cigarette, looked over in Laurie's direction and, blowing out a plume of smoke with his head cocked back, pitched his voice pointedly at him and said, 'Now, Laylah, get down on your knees.'

Laylah commenced crouching. Laurie's buried face released a stifled shriek of torment and Barry let loose a peal of laughter. Traumatised by the proceedings, Laurie gasped convulsively and swooned with shock.

Barry gripped Laylah's wrists and drew her up. 'No need for now. It looks as if he's passed out. Maybe we'll save that for when he comes to so I can savour seeing him squirm,' he guffawed with Laylah joining in. He dragged on his cigarette and then thrust it to the floor, crushing it beneath his boot as he looked at Laurie contemplatively.

He strode to the couch, picked up Laylah's bra and turned Laurie over. He was not completely unconscious and was squinting warily at Barry.

Barry placed its cups over Laurie's eyes and, pressing them down maliciously, said, 'There…there's something for you to contemplate as you take in the sweet smell of a woman's body – my woman. What a pleasure it'll be to have that body – every little bit of it – just as she'll go wild with pleasure having mine. Isn't that right, Lay?' He squatted down to Laurie's ear and asked him in a lowered voice, 'Can you hear me?'

He got no response and so shook Laurie while repeating the question. Laurie moaned.

'Good. You think the world of Laylah, don't you? Really care for her. I'm gonna do whatever I want with her, have my fun and use her up. Then, when I get sick of her, maybe in a month, maybe six, maybe a year, I'm gonna throw her away like a piece of trash. Trash! I just want you to know that.' He got up and said to Laylah, 'Come on, this guy bores me, let's go to bed.'

As they exited, she turned to Laurie and said tauntingly, 'You're welcome to join us if you're inclined.'

'Wicked girl,' Barry sniggered, slapping her rump to hurry her along.

The torrid moans and sighs that wafted from Laurie's bedroom roused him back to full wakefulness. He lay in agony trying his best to stop his ears to the crescendo of lewd exclamations and climactic shrieking assaulting them.

A swirl of thoughts and feelings washed over him like a muddy torrent churning chaotically as it swept away what little clarity his tormented mind still retained. In his turmoil, he was harried by a humiliation that made him feel absolutely worthless and a bitter disgust for the pointless cruelty of life, its merciless allowance of the wantonness of men like Barry, the inevitable corruption of anything unblemished and beautiful like Laylah and, most poignantly, the unedifying weakness of men like himself.

Amid these lacerating thoughts there arose a strange sensation foreign to him, something overwhelming he had never experienced but which, however unfamiliar, he understood to be heartbreak. It was a pain whose intensity was unlike anything he could ever have imagined, so that the tears now running down his cheeks were no longer those induced by choking on alcohol but by grief.

A feeling of rising nausea welled up in him. He forced himself to his feet and staggered to the kitchen, where he leaned over the sink and threw up. He stooped there awaiting the remnants of his stomach to evacuate with each spasm until he was left dry retching. Panting wearily, quiescence finally ensued and as he prepared to return to the couch his eyes fell on a carving knife Rosanna had left in the dish rack to dry. He stretched out his hand and fondled it wistfully, running his index finger over the handle and then the blade. Resting his body on his elbow, he picked it up and with trance-like abstractedness, clasped it in both hands and placed it to his chest.

'There's only one way to end this nightmare,' he heard a voice say, uncertain if it was his or someone else's. 'With your extinction, hers must follow.'

'But will it? Are you sure?' he asked out loud in perplexity.

'Anyway, you're already dead and have nothing left of yourself left to kill,' the voice responded.

He giggled stupidly, stopped abruptly with a distracted look and heard the voice continue, 'You're a chrysalis that has served its purpose and she's the butterfly that left it behind…'

His emaciated face assumed a look of composed resolution whose pointed disengagement from everything around him seemed to suggest the mind behind its expression was no longer in command of its faculties.

'Then I'll kill her!' he whispered as if he'd hit upon a solution so altogether simple and sensible. 'Barry too – kill them both! It really doesn't matter to someone who's already dead how many others join him. Oh, the pretty noise they make. Yes, yes, Laurie will join in the fun and show them how he can make them shriek and howl too. What happy sounds we'll – ugh – make together…'

A sensation of oozing fluid enveloped his hands. It trickled down his arms in crooked streams and dripped off his elbows. Leaning over the sink, he became curiously aware of how sticky the fingers clasped about the knife at his chest had become with thick, warm fluid as he watched it pooling on the counter and spilling over onto the vomit.

Collapsing to his knees, he whispered, 'Blood is thick– Ahh… I must ask Roz to tidy up…'

www.ingramcontent.com/pod-product-compliance
Lightning Source LLC
Chambersburg PA
CBHW021335190726
48288CB00003B/1127